ANIMAL PLANET

ANIMAL PLANET

SCOTT BRADFIELD

PICADOR USA
NEW YORK

Portions of this novel originally appeared in *Conjunctions* and *Triquarterly*.

ANIMAL PLANET. Copyright © 1995 by Scott Bradfield. All rights reserved. Printed in the United States of America. No part of this book may be used or reproduced in any manner whatsoever without written permission except in the case of brief quotations embodied in critical articles or reviews. For information, address Picador USA, 175 Fifth Avenue, New York, N.Y. 10010

Picador® is a U.S. registered trademark and is used by St. Martin's Press under license from Pan Books Limited.

Design by Pei Loi Koay

Library of Congress Cataloging-in-Publication Data

Bradfield, Scott.
 Animal planet / Scott Bradfield.
  p. cm.
  ISBN 0-312-13428-2 (trade cloth)
  1. Animals—Fiction. I. Title.
 PS3552.R214A82 1995
 813'.54—dc20   95-21675
                                                      CIP

First Picador USA Edition: October 1995
10 9 8 7 6 5 4 3 2 1

TO EMMA, WITH LOVE

I think I could turn and live with animals,
* they are so placid and self-contained . . .*
They do not sweat and whine about their condition,
They do not lie awake in the dark and weep for their sins,
They do not make me sick discussing their duty to God,
Not one is dissatisfied . . .

—WALT WHITMAN

PART 1

ANIMALS BEHIND BARS

1

THE WINTER HOLIDAY

Strangely enough, it's in a zoo that animals forget their own community. The closer they're shoved together, the further their minds retreat from themselves. Divided by barred walls that don't hide them, they become afraid of looking into one another's eyes, or listening to one another's words. They ignore the human crowds that visit them, and avoid their own reflections in the glistening water troughs and aluminum food trays. As they grow old together in the same divided spaces, they begin looking forward to only two things—rain and sleep. Because both bring places to hide. Places animals can hide from themselves.

London Zoo was no exception, and eventually, sometime during his middle years, Charlie the Crow went there to rest for a while. Charlie had been flying all his life, seeing many things, and exploring many options. He had been to Asia, Africa, Alaska, and the North Pole. He had seen overcrowded cities, polluted oceans, animal killing fields, corrupted body politics, and an entire solar system's worth of bad faith and fiscal inequality. These days, Charlie just wanted to settle down somewhere. He wanted a place where he could cease moving, but never cease talking. Because Charlie loved to talk. It was one of his life's few pleasures.

"You guys are a trip, man. You really are." Charlie would perch upon a large, smog-stained oak tree in the middle of the compound, and look everybody over with an incurable smugness. "You got your four walls, don't you, Buds? You got your pumped-in muzak, fresh meat and greens, weekly hose downs, and even, when you're good, they might throw you a bone or two. You been cared for so long, you guys think it's your natural condition. It's not that you've grown fat and lazy. It's that you don't have any imagination left anymore. The imagination nature granted you in the first place, like the color of your hair or the number of your limbs. I'm talking about the ability to dream better lives for yourselves than this, you know, this goddamn *zoo*. So what do you guys have to say for yourselves, huh? Are you listening to a single goddamn word I'm trying to tell you or what?"

All across London Zoo, animals regularly heard the words Charlie told them, but couldn't believe those words were meant for them. Turtles, macaws, penguins, and rhinoceri. Swinging baboons, lanky jungle cats, bottled amphibians, and slow cephalapods. Words were used to make animals *do* things, not think about them. Go here. Do that. Eat this. Stop that. So far as the zoo's official residents were concerned, Charlie was perched high above their heads in a way that was not merely physical.

After all, Charlie was a bird.

Charlie could *fly*.

Winter came early that year, and the animals began hearing a lot of *R* words they couldn't pronounce. Words like *recession,*

4

redundancy, and *rationalization.* They heard rumors of lever-aged buyouts, corporate takeovers, asset stripping, privatization, the ECU, Princess Di's mood swings, and the planet-wide biodi-versity crisis. The zoo personnel began to look more pale and unraveled than usual. They didn't sweep the grounds as often, or disinfect the living quarters as thoroughly. Using temperature as an excuse, many animals retreated into plasterboard caverns, set-ting their hibernal clocks for quarter-to-spring. Others fattened their jackets with rich nuts and refined white breads, feeling their blood slow and their ruminations thicken. The crowds of human visitors ebbed. The voices of their human children grew increas-ingly irritable and plaintive.

"Why don't they *do* anything, Mum? Why do they just sit there? And where are the giraffes hiding? Where are all the ele-phants?"

The giant pandas caught cold and went to the hospital.

The shedding snakes hid underneath rocks and logs in slow, greedy ceremonies of digestion.

The solitary okapi, one of the shyest animals in the entire zoo, began weeping uncontrollably at the slightest provocation.

Wanda the Gorilla sat in her cage all day being steadfastly dis-regarded by her massive, emotionally unsupportive mate, Roy. "All I ever do anymore is eat," Wanda complained, tearing apart celery stalks and devouring them into fibrous bits. "I just sit here all day getting fatter and fatter, dropping baby after baby. So tell me—is this any sort of life for a lady?"

The tiger paced in his cage, back and forth, back and forth, while children outside the plate-glass barrier raced him from one end to another. "Just one," he prayed to himself, "and I swear I'll never ask for anything else ever again. Just a little one without too much hair. That's all I'll ever need to be happy."

Only Scaramangus the Wildebeest managed to endure every emotional vicissitude, even those engendered by bad weather.

5

Standing proudly among the females he was born to service and protect, Scaramangus basked in the steam and heat of his own magnificent presence. King of the Beasts. Idol of Men.

"I am chosen," Scaramangus exclaimed proudly every morning when the sparse crowds came. "I am incomparable. I am blessed. From out of all the countless wildebeests in the entire jungle, human beings have chosen *me* to represent my species to the world."

The animals lived their collective lives the only way they knew how. By going along with the rhythm of their secret selves. And by totally ignoring one another.

All day long Charlie the Crow sat on the high wires and looked down at them.

There but for the grace of God, Charlie thought.

It was as if the entire Animal Planet was slumbering.

And nobody on it was ever going to wake up.

2

RADIO ALARM

Then, one night in bleak November, a radical-extremist guerrilla faction of Animal Action! blew the front gate off the zoo with Semtex and dynamite caps. They were wearing black wool ski masks, black jeans, black turtleneck T-shirts, and black leather gloves, like a team of down-market ninjas. Within moments they had disconnected the zoo's various overhead video monitors, burglar alarms, and outside telephones. A series of smaller explosions sounded; cages came unsprung, *pop pop pop*. Then, as casually as if he was flagging a cab, the leader of the guerrilla band raised a triumphant fist to the moon blond sky.

"We all breathe the air!" he cried. "We all love the earth! Endangered species of the world—unite!"

The black-clad guerrillas leapt back over the turnstiles and disappeared into Regent's Park, bobbing and weaving across the green fields as if pursued by enemy sniper fire.

The entire zoo was suddenly dark again, silent, preemptive, dense.

And everybody sat up dazedly in their ruptured enclosures, waiting for something that had already happened.

"Mama mia!" chirped Charlie the Crow, perched atop one of the recently embattled ticket kiosks. "Holy bloody cow."

Charlie could hardly contain himself. He performed a little salsa on the kiosk's slate roof.

Something was happening, he thought.

And for once it was something he hadn't even begun to anticipate.

Charlie dove into the shining air. A fine mist sprayed his face; the cool conflux of moonlight hummed. Across the zoo's triangular, compartmentalized map, the animals were slowly awakening to one another.

"Caw caw," Charlie told them. "Caw caw caw caw."

The wolves sniffed at their broken, wrought-iron gate. Retreated, conferred, sniffed again. The prospect of freedom made them wary. A little uncertain about who they wanted to be.

For some, however, doubt never entered their minds. Wanda the Gorilla took one look at her husband, Roy, and she knew.

Already asleep again, he was picking his nose and snoring. Wanda tossed a half-eaten apple over one shoulder and swung through the open door.

Anywhere, she thought. Except where I already am.

Charlie turned and turned again. Movements, smells, new awarenesses, old routines being casually forgotten. In their hay-strewn domiciles, even the slumbering elephants were beginning to rouse. I am not asleep, the elephants thought. The world is changing and I am not asleep.

To his amazement, Charlie saw a community of animals beginning to take shape. Ruminants, primates, rodents, carnivores, and marsupials. Wild ground squirrels and golden lion tamarinds, meerkats and mongooses, fennec foxes and old spotted pigs. The animals were journeying into the strange, neutral spaces between their cages. They were seeing their own freedom reflected in the eyes of everybody else.

We are all different, they realized.

And yet all somehow the same.

The animals assembled in the amphitheater, where chimps had activated the sound system, and by the time Charlie got there the amplifiers were wailing with feedback. In response, the animals joined their discordant voices into one terrific jungle clamor.

With a swoop and a flourish, Charlie snapped up the mike from Wanda, who was fruitlessly trying to incite the crowd with tales of her husband Roy's ruthless banana consumption.

"You know what you guys sound like?" Charlie shouted. "You sound like a bunch of *animals!*"

Charlie's strangely familiar voice sent a hush over the crowd.

For the first time in their lives, the animals realized what hadn't even been conceivable before. Someone was speaking to *them*. And they were supposed to *listen*.

"You guys want to say something? Then say it in *words,* man, not grunts and roars. Be goddamn articulate, will you, because you've got a choice in this world, whether you like it or not. You either learn to make sense of your lives, or somebody else makes sense of them for you. And where does that leave you, my fellow beasties? I'll tell you where that leaves you. Right back there where you came from. Sitting in cages, man. Pissing on your own doorsteps."

The animals heard a strange, collective voice begin to emerge from their throats. One long, gathering note of disquiet, anguish, and terrible remorse.

"Now, for the first time in your far-too-miserable lives, you've got a chance to speak for yourselves," Charlie told them. "You can form your own government, make your own laws, relearn your own culture. Haven't you guys seen *Spartacus?* Haven't you guys seen *The Battle for Algiers?*"

"Spih, spih, *spih,* " hissed the sibilant snakes.

"Al-*geesh,* " sneezed the white pelicans. "Al-*geesh, geesh!*"

Charlie shrugged off the momentary lapse of momentum.

"Okay, maybe not. But you don't need to watch telly to know you're being robbed of your freedom! Stay in your little cage, they tell you. That way you won't be *exterminated!* What sort of reasoning is that? I'll tell you what sort of reasoning it is. It's malevolent, genocidal, terra-phobic, uncompromising right-brain-thinking human aggression—*that's* what it is! And have we had enough? I'm asking *you* guys? Have *we* had *enough?*"

It wasn't even a word at first. Just a low swerve of vowels. Affirmative. Regular. Long.

"I can't *hear* you!" Charlie cried. "What are you—dumb animals or *wild beasts of the jungle?* Let me hear it, guys! *Who's* had enough? *Who's* sick of being lied to? *Who's* ready to take control of their lives?"

And then it was a word. Intact. Hard. Anchored to the special reality of their intimate animal selves.

"Us!" the animals roared. "Us, us, us, us, *us!*"

3

THE SPIRIT OF THE AGE

(Us. Us.)

Scaramangus the Wildebeest was the last animal to awaken, starting to his feet with a gasp and blinking at the distant blue lights of the auditorium.

Not us, Scaramangus thought to himself. Not us, but *them*.

By the time Scaramangus reached the front entrance, the animals were piling picnic tables and broken lumber against the gates, feverishly turning their idea of the zoo inside out. Someone had started a small bonfire in one of the litter bins. Someone else had overturned the refrigerated cabinets in the Raffles Bar and Restaurant, where animals were riotously sucking on frozen hotdogs and fistfuls of gluey pizza dough.

Scaramangus, meanwhile, stood proudly among them, refusing to get involved. These, he thought, were noisy animals. These were animals without any sense of decorum. Worst of all, these were animals who only pretended not to notice him. Then, the moment Scaramangus let his guard down, *bam!* Meat for somebody else's stew.

Slowly Scaramangus grew aware of a pair of steady eyes trained upon his haunches.

"Hey there, Mister," the voice behind him said.

This was not the Great Society, Scaramangus knew. This was just the same old jungle, where only the strong survived.

He turned, pawed the ground, and breathed his contempt into the chill air. This was the challenge. The supreme test was now.

Wanda the Gorilla had adorned herself in a torn floppy sun hat, terry-cloth leg warmers, and a large green plastic rain poncho liberated from one of the trash bins. The poncho was swung low to reveal a glimpse of hairy cleavage.

"I say, darling. Have we met?" Wanda batted her eyelashes and offered him the last bits of a Kit Kat from her chocolatey fingers. "Are you an antelope or something? I dig those horns."

Scaramangus took another, even deeper breath.

"I," Scaramangus reminded her, "am a wildebeest. The proudest, and mightiest, and most handsome on the face of the Animal Planet."

Wanda's eyes widened.

"Oh *really?*" Wanda replied. "So tell me this, then. Where have you *been* all my life, huh?"

Dawn didn't approach. It gradually pervaded.

First the helicopters arrived; then a siege of police vans, bomb disposal squads, and BBC news minicams. "Please, we know you're upset," Superintendent Heathcliff declared over his new lightweight megaphone. "Who wouldn't be? But why can't we talk this thing over face to face? We're only here to *help.*"

The Superintendent was wearing a crisp, white short-sleeve shirt and pleated, navy blue cotton slacks.

"Lousy bastards," Charlie sighed. "I knew they'd try a little false compassion first, just to loosen us up. Those lying heathen will stoop to just about *any*thing!"

"Look, we realize you big animals can take care of your-selves," Superintendent Heathcliff continued. "But think about the little ones—the tarsiers, say, or even the cute little penguins. They're pretty far down the old food chain, wouldn't you say? Another night's sleep among the rest of you meat eaters and, well. Let's face it. An unregulated zoo can get pretty messy."

Charlie could feel the mood of the assembled animals starting to turn. Jungle cats were glancing over their shoulders at lone pigs and yearlings. The cliquish wolves were conferring in whispers, observing a twitching orange huddle of dormice.

"When we need human intervention to settle our quarrels, we'll *ask* for it!" Charlie cried back.

"Give us a chance," the Superintendent said. "We *want* to improve your standard of living, but at the same time we've *got* to be fiscally responsible. We're working on a lot of new ideas right now, but we'll need *your* help to implement them."

"For example," Charlie said.

"Well, market forces. We open up the zoo to what they call Free Enterprise Zones. We farm you out to extracurricular jobs— serving tea for the handicapped, fetching groceries and newspapers, or a little rudimentary shop and construction work. We give you all an individual opportunity to improve your lives through hard work and competitive negotiation. And just between you and me, Mr. Crow, what sort of animals do you think might benefit from such a scheme? Well, those with opposable thumbs are going to clean up, of course. But a bright bird such as yourself, who's mastered the fundamentals of human speech and grammar—let's just say that such a hypothetical bird won't do too badly, either. If you know what I mean?"

"Yeah, *right.*" Charlie was pacing irritably back and forth on a strand of rusty barbed wire. "You mean you'll put us on overcrowded tubes and trains every day, other people sneezing on us, no air-conditioning. You'll tax the bones out of us and instead of investing it in animal services, you'll spend it to subsidize the chemical and weapons industries. Look, buster, do you really think we'll fall for this bogus 'market forces' folderol? We may be animals—but that doesn't mean we're *stupid!*"

The animals, startled by their own abrupt consensus, roared.

The trees shook.

The sky expanded with oxygen and light.

"Well, don't say I didn't warn you," concluded the handsome Superintendent. "Because there are others in my department who aren't so sympathetic to public insurrection. If you want to talk this thing over at *any* time, just ask for me, Superintendent Heathcliff. And let me wish you all the best of luck. You're going to need it."

4

FREE LABOR, FREE SOIL

From that point on, it was only a matter of time. The animals had already gorged themselves on all the best junk food and candy bars. They had already sprayed graffiti across the walls of the Caretaker's office and public restrooms. FREEDOM OR DEATH! ANIMAL RIGHTS NOW! FREE THE SERENGHETI SEVEN! EAT THE RICH BEFORE THEY EAT YOU! The animals knew they had done all they could. They had uttered the truth as articulately as their crude tongues allowed.

"If every animal could journey into space on an orbital satellite, they would experience the same revelation." Charlie was sucking warm Tetley's out of a pint-sized aluminum can, feeling lethargic and sentimental. "They would look into the same darkness. They would see the same reflected light of the sun, illuminating the Animal Planet in all its glory. A bit of blue-green mold, pear shaped, slowly spinning. The fragile, momentary testament of it. Forests broken and slashed. Cities stupefied by their own poisonous emissions. The blue waters turning gray and disconsolate in patches. Each animal would feel him- or herself diminish into this expanding awareness of our entire planet. Not a sense of responsibility, really. Just a sense of location. A grounding in space and time. Each animal would come plummeting back to earth with a feeling of incorporation. Knowing that we are all part of the same enterprise, and that it's not owned by AMEX or Dow Jones. A tiny planet packed with countless blundering and unsatisfiable animals, trying to help each other out the best we can. This, friends, is my dream. When I fly, this is the dream that sustains me."

They came in the late afternoon, a time reserved for the animals' second feeding. The wet plop of teargas canisters drew arcs of smoke across the blue sky, and snipers fired hypodarts from elevated cranes and rooftops.

The largest animals fell first, feeling the barbiturates bite into their flanks and haunches. Panicked, the remaining animals stampeded wildly, blinded by the gas, knocking over fences and water fountains, trampling one another into the boiling gray dust.

For Scaramangus, the line between himself and the other animals suddenly vanished, threatening to take him with it. The chaos of bodies, the random brutality and anguish, the feverish clash of animals and men. A truncheon glanced off Scaramangus's forehead and he staggered, turned.

Scaramangus tried to cry out, "Stop! You don't know who I am!"

Then the Riot Officer lifted his truncheon again. Wearing a

hideous off-green gas mask, he resembled a cross between an aardvark and an elephant.

"You don't even know my name, or whose side I'm on," Scaramangus cried. "I might as well be an ocelot, or a rat, or a parakeet so far as you're concerned." Scaramangus couldn't believe these were his words on his lips.

A big fat alligator, Scaramangus thought, watching the truncheon descend. A cheetah, a reindeer, a centipede, or a finch.

The truncheon continued to descend. Time, Scaramangus thought. Terrible time.

The sky wasn't blue anymore.

The truncheon came down.

For the next week to ten days, the animals were kept tranquilized in their cages and enclosures. They weren't allowed to frequent the exercise yards or the children's petting zoo. They were fed more cereal and less meat. Every day the wind blew scraps of morning newspaper into their cages, and the animals perused them for articles about their brief fling with greatness. But the newspapers mentioned only shifting interest rates, Third World death squads, American tobacco exports to Thailand. There was hardly any animal news in them whatsoever.

Superintendent Heathcliff was now acting as interim Head Caretaker, assigned to oversee the zoo's imminent foreclosure.

"Well," the new Head Caretaker announced one day, his voice, as always, eminently reasonable and firm. "I tried to warn you, didn't I? I told you we were facing some pretty severe economic shortfalls around this place—you can't expect the public to continue paying your bills *forever,* can you? What it comes down to is this—I'm afraid we'll be closing the zoo in September, so most of you guys will have to be relocated right away. I think the change of climate can only do you all a world of good."

Charlie had taken up roost on Scaramangus's gate, but Scaramangus, having received unusually large dosages of quaaludes over the past few days, didn't seem to notice.

"Trick is," Charlie continued, "you can't cage an entire nation. You can only cage individual animals, one or two at a time. Ergo, a competitive economy. Animal versus animal, male versus female, the have-somes versus the have-nones. Don't let them fool you with their bullshit about economic retrenchment, Scary. What's being retrenched is us. Because we're bigger together than we are apart—and don't you forget it."

Scaramangus was dimly aware of Charlie chattering away on the wire fence. But everything seemed smaller, frailer, and more fragile than before the revolution.

"Maybe the Japs are right," Charlie jabbered, pacing back and forth on the wire. "Maybe we *are* witnessing an era that has given up on the idea of history altogether. The sense that we are shaping a collective future, and that we owe debts and responsibilities not only to the corporations who pay our salaries but to the planetary forces that loan us this flesh in which we're wrapped. I think it's a very difficult time to be living, Scary. No matter what they tell us in the newspapers, I think it's a pretty difficult time, indeed."

Scaramangus lifted himself unsteadily to his feet and shivered the dust from his jacket. He shook his face, trying to pump blood into his brain and loosen his lips.

Out in the zoo's central arena, the Head Caretaker was speaking over the microphone to an assembly of local businessmen and community leaders who had come to make bids on the soon-to-be disenfranchised animals.

"And as for the first order of the day," the Head Caretaker announced cheerfully, "we have a very, very special young lady we'd like you all to meet. Bring her out, boys, so the gentlemen can see."

Wanda, stripped down to one forlorn, bruised banana, was resting her forehead against the bars of her portable cage and wheezing softly.

"We're talking about a prime bit of animal real estate here, friends," the Head Caretaker told them. "Almost as smart as a human being—that's our hairy animal cousin, the mighty black gorilla. Stronger, friendlier, and better coordinated than any child. They make great exhibits—in the mezzanine of your office building, say. Or at that stockholders' meeting you're planning for the Bahamas next Spring. Let's start this off right. Do I hear one thousand pounds?"

"Maybe, maybe, maybe, maybe," Charlie moaned, over and over again, trying to drown out the Caretaker's magnified voice in his ears.

Suddenly, all the anger Scaramangus had ever felt in his entire life lifted up out of his body and deposited itself on the gate where Charlie was sitting.

"I hear fifteen hundred," the Caretaker declared. "Do I hear seventeen-five?"

Across the zoo, defeated animals felt the weather start to turn. They sat up in their cages and tried to see into the central arena, where the auction platform was surrounded by armed guards.

It was only a word, but Scaramangus knew it. With a sudden roar and a lunge, Scaramangus threw his entire body against the gate and the impact flung Charlie high into the air, wheeling, the earth literally knocked out from under him. Scaramangus reared against the gate with his horns.

It was the word.

The word versus the gate and something had to give.

"Us!" Scaramangus shouted, straining against the bars with his back, his shoulders, his haunches, and his brain. "Us! Us! Us! *Us!*"

17

He backed up. He saw the gate. He saw the world beyond the gate. He saw the overweight men with bad complexions standing in the arena, brushing off their three-piece suits, turning their pale faces toward the word Scaramangus was trying to tell them.

"Us!" Scaramangus cried. And charged the gate again.

Across the zoo the word was lifting them in their cages. It was time. They would say it now.

The animals began to roar.

PART 2

POLAR LATITUDE

1

THE BIG CHILL

The first time Buster heard anything about the London Zoo Rebellion he was engaged in a frosty argument with his wife, Sandy.

"Then you explain it to *me*, Buster." Sandy was showing him a wooden serving spoon, as if it might end up providing his next meal. "If you're so high on your big buddy, Whistling Pete, then why don't *you* explain his behavior to *me*."

This was the part of an argument Buster knew he couldn't win unless Sandy let him—and of course Sandy *never* let him. So he went directly to the large Philco and turned it on, scanning the knobby serrated dial for anything from the BBC World Service.

"Why don't you just cool down, Sandy," he said. "There are two sides to every story, you know."

He dialed through foreign-language pop stations, Australian radio drama, sonar *blips* and *beeps,* and several emergency frequency test broadcasts. Eventually, though, he found something a little more substantial—Paul Harvey on Armed Forces Radio, presenting his daily wrap-up of the news.

"Good day," Paul Harvey said.

"You want to hear two sides to every story?" Sandy was shaking the wooden spoon even more vigorously. "I'll give you two sides to every story, Buster. Whistling Pete's screwed-over wife, Estelle, and his screwed-over kid, Pete Jr. *There's* your two sides to every story."

Buster sat down in his stuffed chair by the fire and gazed at the polished radio. A wedding present from Sandy's family, it had turned out to be the most expensive possession in their upper maisonette ice condo on the Antarctic Peninsula.

"Come on, baby. It's time for the news."

Then, just in the nick of time, Paul Harvey said, "Dateline, London, England. While Americans on the West Coast. Are waking up. To more thundershowers. The English Royal Police Constabulary. Are putting to sleep. A violent rebellion. Within their own borders. I'm talking about the London Zoo. Ladies and gentlemen. I'm talking about lions. Tigers. Elephants. You name it. Taking arms. Against their human. Keepers. And now— page two."

Even Sandy was drawn by the voice on the radio. After only a few moments the wooden spoon hung limply at her side, and her black eyes had that faraway look in them.

"What's a lion, Buster? What's a tiger? But most of all—what's a human being?"

Sandy came and sat down on the footstool beside him.

Absently, Buster took her stubby wing in his lap and stroked it gently. Buster loved to hear about faraway places filled with strange animals he didn't know about, because he believed that if he thought about them long and hard enough, they might fulfill all his vague yearnings. Then he would never have to leave his cozy home in suburban Antarctica.

"Who knows, Sandy? Now shh, please. Let's listen and maybe we'll find out."

2

PENGUINS FOR LUNCH

Buster enjoyed dreaming about strange places, but beyond that he didn't like to get too involved. Which was probably why he was such good friends with his polar opposite, Whistling Pete, a middle-aged penguin who didn't dream so much as *act*. And who subsequently got himself carnally involved with just about every cute penguinette he could lay his flippers on.

Every morning Whistling Pete went to work, punched his time card, and sat in his office stamping requisition forms, acting no different than any other professional, white-collar penguin on Penguin Island. Then, just before the noon whistle blew, he would adjourn to the Gents, apply generous dashes of aftershave to his cheeks and buttocks, and dispatch himself to a series of seedy assignations with various lovely penguinettes from the local business district. Secretaries, account management assistants, receptionists, Gal Fridays, and office temps. For Whistling Pete, lunchtime infidelity occurred as regularly as clockwork. It had become, in fact, a matter of sublime routine.

He met them unashamedly at the Ice Floe Bar & Grill for drinks and quick, hot lunches, while gratuitously proffering flowers, compliments, stockings, and chocolates. Then, as fast as their little legs could carry them, he hurried them next door to the Crystal Palace Motel, where he kept an open account. There they ordered caviar and champagne through room service, sported themselves silly across the taut fitted coverlets, and made the most they could of an hour—sometimes of an hour and a half.

"This is the life," Whistling Pete muttered every so often. "This is what the All-Mighty Penguin had in mind when he designed such cute little penguinettes."

Later they would shower, dress, and depart separately, pretending to be discrete. Then, around three or three-thirty, Whistling Pete would return to his office across the road, already in the grip of a postcoital melancholy that wasn't altogether unpleasant. He felt soft, used, and distinctly unprovocative. He was ready for a long dreamy nap at his desk.

"Hey there, bro," Buster would say, leaning into the office around five-thirty. "We hitting Happy Hour today or what?"

Whistling Pete abruptly sat up in his spring-cocked office chair. He saw the binders and ledgers, the interoffice memos and desk-supply requisition forms.

(And somewhere else entirely: Melody, Martha, Trudy, Dallas, Pippa, Dolores, and Joyce.)

"Buster, old pal," Pete said finally, clapping his wings together with brisk authority, "has the sun stopped shining or the earth ceased to spin? Of *course* we're hitting Happy Hour. And if I recall correctly, it's *your* turn to pick up the tab."

"Domesticity is for the birds," Pete pronounced later, walking home with Buster through the starry night. "Sure, it *sounds* nice and all. Big tract houses, gas central heating, indoor plumbing, and all that. Trade, commerce, low-tech industry, certified schools for the kids, community rep, all the bread in one basket, *that* sort of domesticity, *you* know. But basically, man, it's an idea cooked up by the little girlies. Wives, man. Females seeking security for their babes. Girlies are home builders, but us guys, we're like home *breakers*. It's not our *fault*, Buster. It's just our *nature*."

The long white road descended into the village, leading them toward the smell of yeasty bread baking.

Whistling Pete put his wing around Buster with a comradely squeeze and gestured downhill. "There it is, buddy. Our little village in the snow. Back in the old days our ancestors waddled around on *rocks,* man. They starved, hunted, mated, and died without proper funerals or mortgage insurance. And who do you think initiated the idea of *houses,* man? Why, the *ladies,* of course. 'Let's stack a few ice blocks over here as a sort of lean-to,' they told their weary, flatulent old husbands. 'How about four walls, honey? A roof and a floor?' Us guys would have lain out there scratching our lice on that stupid rock forever if *we'd* had the choice. But the choice *wasn't* ours, man. And never has been."

Buster, well oiled with budget tequila, was waddling along beside Pete with uncustomary resolution, gazing dreamily into the illuminated sky: showers of meteors, swirls of galaxies, planets entrained by moons and whorling dust. Buster loved the night when it got like this: vast, unencompassable, and rinsed with sensation.

"Actually," Buster muttered out loud, "I always kind of dug three square meals, a warm bed, and all that? But when I look out at all those stars, Pete, and all that *space,* it makes me feel, I don't know. Kind of homesick, like for places I've never been."

But Pete wasn't listening to a word Buster said. Instead he was thinking: Melody, Marianne, Gwendolyn, and Jane. Tomorrow at noon and next Wednesday at twelve forty-five.

"Men may *build* the cities," Pete said softly, just before they arrived at his white doorway, his paved driveway, his leaning and personalized mailbox. "But believe you me. It's the little girlies who make us live in them."

By the time Buster arrived home, he found Sandy sitting up in the living room, finishing a tall glass of sherry, and listening to the radio. She didn't look up when he came in. Sometimes,

Buster realized, he and Sandy suffered their worst quarrels when he wasn't around.

"They've been repeating the same words all night, Buster. What does it mean? And who *are* they?"

Buster took his hot cocoa and stood by the fire while a stern, fatherly voice on the radio repeated over and over: "Animals of the world, put down your arms. Animals of the world, let's talk things over. Animals of the world, rebellion is pointless. Animals of the world, we're coming to set you free."

Buster sipped his cocoa and sighed.

"Radio drama?" he ventured. "Kind of like that famous Orson Welles broadcast—*The War of the Worlds?* You think?"

"They keep talking about the London Zoo, Buster. They keep promising it'll never happen again."

Buster couldn't look Sandy in the eye. He was thinking how bound up he was by this house, this mortgage, this life. It all seemed so strange somehow. Like a place he had never been.

"Don't worry too much about what you hear on the radio," he assured her. "Because radio isn't real, Sandy. Radio is only make-believe."

MORDIDA GIRLS

Spring returned and the squat white sun wouldn't leave. Time grew increasingly diffuse, gray and immeasurable.

Not that time mattered to Whistling Pete anymore—only the quick lapse into timelessness he regained every day in the arms of his adorable penguinettes. Often he trysted two or three on a single afternoon, bang bang bang, beginning each session with a few shots of Jack Daniel's and a plate of imported caviar. Then, by the third or fourth session, he fell rudely asleep and dreamed of white, sandy beaches and tropical heat. Later he awoke in the dim room alone, saw the windows hung with thick black curtains, and heard the hissing radiators.

Then, out of the blue, hotel personnel would knock summarily at his plywood door.

"Maid service," said a woman with a heavy Dutch accent. "Should ve clean up, Mister? Or you vant ve should come back later?"

By the time Pete waddled into work, his assistant, Nadine, was usually in a furious temper.

"Mr. Oswald came by from Marketing, and Joe Wozniak asked about your expense receipts again. I've *tried* covering for you as far as the sales conference, but I've got to see some retail brochures pretty damn soon. Oh, and your wife and little boy popped round—seems you were supposed to take your son fishing. They waited nearly an hour, but then they left."

"Oh shit," Whistling Pete said, and slumped into his padded swivel chair. He checked both his vest pockets for stray cigarettes, but located only twisted bits of tobacco and one small white business card. The card said:

HENRIETTA PHILPOTT

PUBLIC RELATIONS CONSULTANT

He wondered if he and Henrietta had spent any time together. Or if maybe they were about to.

"I *knew* I forgot something," Whistling Pete said.

Pete continued making excuses, but even he didn't want to hear them anymore.

"I'm *going* to take Junior fishing," Pete declared. "It's just I got *delayed* meeting a distributor from the Stroud Islands. What do you want me to do—neglect my job?"

"I sure wouldn't want that," Estelle said emptily, leaning against the kitchen table. "Obviously neglecting your *job's* all you're worried about anymore. So tell that to your year-old son who adores you."

"I'll make it up to you, sport, I really will." Pete paced back and forth in the living room while Junior lay on the floor perusing his geography homework *(Fishing Routes of Our Polar World, Twelfth Edition)*. "We'll go camping, that's it. A weekend on the South Orkneys. Just you, me, and those mackerel. We'll bring along that new sealskin pup tent we've been meaning to try out."

Junior didn't look up. He tapped a pencil against his beak, and turned the page of his textbook.

"Like, that's *cool,* Dad. We'll go fishing some other time. When you're not so busy, that is."

"I've *got* the expense receipts," Pete told the Executive Staff in the Factory Green Room. "Of *course* I've got the expense receipts." The Executive Directors had called him in during lunch break, where they sat around the long black conference table, munching processed-salmon sandwiches and prawn-flavored crisps.

"It's just that, well, Payroll screwed up the Group Finance Report, and by the time Nadine and I got that mess straightened out with the Commissary, it was time for the Monthly Service Catalog, and, well, I *know* it sounds like a bunch of half-assed excuses and all . . ."

A bright cold sweat broke out on Pete's face and he felt a faint dizzying rush, as if he were falling through vortices of warm air.

". . . and of *course* I'll get the reports to you by Friday, and I don't like to sound like I'm trying to divert blame or anything, right, 'cause of course Nadine's a great girl and all, but she *does* have something of an attitude problem. I mean, like, she's always blaming everything on the *system,* right, and the male-dominated patriarchy and all that, and, well, it's sort of hard to get Nadine to cooperate so far as her official duties are concerned. I'm not *blaming* Nadine for all the screwups, understand. I'm just saying there's only so much *I* can do about them."

Some nights, finding the bedroom door bolted shut, Pete knocked politely like a timid solicitor.

"Estelle?"

"What?"

"Are you in there?"

"Of course I'm in here."

"Can I come in?"

"No you can't."

"I'm really bushed, Estelle. I need to lie down."

"So sleep on the couch."

"I feel very strange, you know, all run down and everything. I've got stomach pains, my liver's enlarged, there may even be something wrong with my spleen. I've got a rash on my inner thigh that burns like crazy. I'm really beat, Estelle, and I think, well. Maybe we should talk."

"There's nothing to talk about," Estelle said calmly, as if she were slipping a form letter under the door. "I'm afraid the time for talking is over."

Whistling Pete leaned against the wall. He could detect her warmth in there, like radium. It felt very far away.

"Oh Estelle," Pete sighed, feeling his entire body slump into itself like an expiring party balloon. "Maybe you're right, honey. Maybe you're right."

Later that same night, in another part of the suburb, Buster sat up in bed watching moonlight through the window and hearing engines in the dark. He was sleeping in the guest room, and Sandy hadn't been speaking to him for nearly two days.

A series of silver military airplanes was flying over Penguin Island, spilling thousands of sheets of white printed paper in its wake. Buster could sense the pieces of paper fluttering high in the air, even without seeing them. He didn't even need to get out of bed, pull on his robe and slippers, and go outside.

But he did.

He got dressed and went outside.

The moonlight was everywhere, and drifts of white paper lay across the tiny village like a weird precipitation.

And each sheet of paper said the same thing:

WE ARE COMING TO SAVE YOU
YOU HAVE NOTHING TO FEAR BUT YOURSELVES

4

THE CRYSTAL PALACE MOTEL

A few weeks later, Buster sat at the Ice Floe Bar & Grill sipping a strawberry margarita while Al the portly bartender swabbed everything down with a damp dishcloth.

"He's been over there every night," Al said. He shifted a toothpick from one side of his beak to the other, and nodded in the direction of the Crystal Palace Motel. "Every day *and* night, actually. And when he comes in here, usually for another bottle of Schmirnoff's, he doesn't say hi or anything. He just takes what he needs and leaves."

"No skin off my butt," Buster said, gargling a shard of ice in his gullet. "He obviously doesn't need *my* help anymore. He's got his little girlies to keep him company."

"Little girlies," Al said, and poured himself a soda water from the hand dispenser. "Little girlies and God knows what else."

It was three P.M. and Buster had just finished a late lunch of oysters in clam sauce.

"And God knows what else," Al said again.

He refused to look at Buster, and there was something in this refusal that Buster took as a reproach.

After lunch and a second margarita, Buster tried calling Pete's room at the Crystal Palace Motel, but there wasn't any answer. When he stopped by the lobby, he found the day clerk playing a new handheld electronic ice hockey game. The day clerk swung the beeping computer toy back and forth, as if he were steering a particularly nasty slalom down the rocky hillside of his imagination.

"Is Whistling Pete still in Room Four-oh-eight?" Buster asked. Buster lit a fresh cigarette off the old one and crushed the old one out in a hip-high, sand-filled aluminum ashtray.

"Ah shit," the day clerk said.

The computer beeped its tiny contempt.

"Whistling Pete, huh?" He gave Buster the once-over. "He's not the sort of guy who has many friends. So you must be another customer, right?"

Before he knew it, Buster was lifting the stroppy, bell-hatted little penguin up over the countertop and slamming him rudely against the clattery ashtray.

"What's *that* supposed to mean, numb nuts?"

"Hey, I was just kidding, is all. Cool it, okay?"

Then Buster heard a tone in his own voice that he didn't recognize.

"I'll ask you one more time, and don't give me any blather. Where can I find my friend Whistling Pete?"

"Well, it's not paradise," Pete conceded. "But then, who's looking for paradise, right?" He was sitting on the edge of his frayed, sunken mattress, scratching his genitals through his checkered boxer shorts. The motel room was littered with bottles, newspapers, and crumpled fast-food wrappers.

"Why don't you take a shower, Pete? Put on some clean underwear, for godsakes. Then I'll take you home to your wife and kid."

"My wife and kid are history, Buster. Estelle took Junior to her sister's on the Fimbulisen Ice Shelf."

Buster refused to be deterred. If Pete was to ever have faith in himself again, Buster would have to be the one who taught him how.

"First we'll get you squared away," Buster said. "Then we'll go bring her back."

"Bring her back to what?" Pete picked a white sticky substance from his ear and wiped it on the mottled sheets. "What's left of me ain't exactly a work of art, you know. And you must have heard about the expense money I embezzled. Nadine getting fired for *my* incompetence and graft. The fact that I've lost what little reputation and self-respect I had left. And the funny thing is, I don't give a goddamn, 'cause I don't miss any of it. Especially not the self-respect."

Embarrassed, Buster looked away. He saw the messy bath-room; the broken, dripping toilet; towels on the floor; stains on the drapes.

"We'll find you a new job," Buster said. "With Estelle and Junior's help we'll get you back on your feet again. Hell, buddy, *I* can loan you a few bob till you get yourself straightened out. What are friends for?"

"Oh Buster," Pete sighed. "Wake up and smell the coffee, will you?" Pete indicated his entire body with a small ironic flourish. The high strain of ribs, the frazzled patchy feathers, the haunted and thinning gleam in his eyes. "All my nice sleek body fat has melted away. No job, no family, no savings to speak of. It's quite ironic, really. Because civilization has given me the luxury of thinking, I've had time to disrespect all the civilized comforts that allow me to think."

"Don't," Buster said. He knew he was in trouble if Pete started talking. "Stop it, Pete. Stop winding yourself up."

Pete was on his feet again, waddling back and forth in front of the bed. "But *that's* the point, isn't it? What do you build when you build yourself a civilization? Nice warm houses, nice warm restaurants, nice warm places to go to the bathroom. What does civilization give us, Buster? Temperature. Heat. Oxygen. Light. And what do we do with all this, this *energy,* this year-round fat and reserve? We burn it, pal. We use it to stoke the fire of our own bodies all day and all night. We are burners of hard fuel, Buster, and thinkers of hard thoughts, and we can't ever rest until we die. Civilization doesn't solve problems, Buster. It reminds us of all the problems we haven't yet solved. What we don't have. Who we haven't been. How much we haven't spent. How many little girlies we haven't plugged. It doesn't end, Buster. I keep thinking it *will* end, but it never *does.*"

"Don't do this to yourself," Buster said desperately. "Turn it *off,* man. Shut your damn brain *off.*"

Pete's eyes were lit with a fire that burned themselves as much as the things they saw.

"But Buster," he said. "The only way to turn off who you are is to pretend not to be."

At which point Whistling Pete fell to the floor with a terrible crash.

They buried Whistling Pete in the pond where he first went fishing with his father. A lid was cut in the ice and Pete's naked body inserted into the frothy, secret currents beneath. On the fringes of the small crowd a few lonely, heavily veiled penguinettes sobbed quietly into black satin handkerchiefs.

Once the lid of ice was refitted into place, a few words were said by each of Pete's surviving friends and relatives. Usually they offered slow, awkward condolences, like "He will be missed," or "He was always a hard worker and good provider," with a dull casual flourish, as if they were signing a form letter. The last person to take the mound was Pete's father, who had swum in that morning from his retirement village on Canary Island. (Pete's mother had died two years previously in a freak skiing accident.)

"Whistling Pete was a good boy," his father said in a cracked, halting voice, trying to read from a sheet of foolscap in his trembling hands. He wore a faded gray flannel shirt, a black wool stocking cap, and wire-rim bifocals. "He was always polite to his parents, did well in school, and helped his mother with the housework. Now maybe he exaggerated the truth every once in a while, but that's just the way he was. He found the truth a little boring, so he tried to embellish it a little; it was kind of like generosity. Maybe some people considered it selfish. But I always thought he just gave life everything he had because he loved it so much."

Abruptly, Mr. Pete began to sob, and a hush fell over the mourners.

Buster stepped up and whispered something in Mr. Pete's ear.

"No, no, I'm *okay,*" Mr. Pete declared, and shook his sheet of foolscap at Buster as if he were shooing flies. Then he wiped his glasses with the end of his stocking cap, folded the foolscap in half, and slipped it into his vest pocket.

"I just wanted to say that Whistling Pete was always polite to his mother and father when he was little, and that's how I'll always remember him."

5

THE LAND OF THE MIDNIGHT SUN

In the renewed silence of their coop-duplex apartment, Buster and Sandy maintained a tender, almost obstinate parity.

"No, sweetheart," Buster would demur, leaning to grant her a kiss behind each ear. "This is *my* night to do the dishes. *You* washed up two nights in a row *last* week."

They sat in the living room every evening after dinner sipping Darjeeling, nibbling oven-hot gingerbread, and listening to the BBC World Service. Old empires disintegrating in the Baltic, the Adriatic, the Sahara, South Africa, Taiwan. Currencies crashing and stock markets rocketing. The pose and strut of presidents, businessmen, pretenders, and kings. "Before civilization," Whistling Pete used to say, "we never had time to realize how much we didn't have. Now we've got all the time in the world to worry about what we'll never keep." Ever since the funeral, Buster often felt Pete's voice sneaking up behind him like a simple memory of resonance.

Some nights he lay awake in bed and listened to the jets passing overhead. Every so often the apartment shook with the reverberant clap of the sound barrier being broken one more time.

"They're building up the McMurdo naval base," he told Sandy while she snored, "arriving on massive flagships and aircraft carriers. They're installing nuclear waste dumps, oil refineries, radio stations, and military barracks. They're going to keep coming even when they don't know what's out here. They're going to keep coming until there's nowhere left for them to go."

In the mornings before work Buster took long aimless walks into the wilderness, wrapped tightly in his sealskin parkas and scratchy woolen underdrawers. He knew this was the dream Pete had died trying to realize, and that if he tried to realize it himself, then he would have to die, too. Not a dream of comfort or plenitude, but a sort of homeless insufficiency. Buster ascended mountains and forded rivers. He skated across plains of ice and refraction, hopping from one jaggedy landmass to another. Some mornings he got lost and arrived late for work, eventually receiving three unofficial warnings and one official reprimand. One more tardy report or no-show, they told him, and he would be fired. No explanations asked.

That night at home, Sandy tried to understand.

"Do you know what you're doing?" she asked. Sandy had lit soft candles and was preparing a cheese soufflé. She was wearing a string of pearls, rubber pedal pushers, and a Dacron shower cap—a combination she knew looked really good on her.

"Not really," Buster said. He sat beside the fireplace and waited. He didn't know what he was waiting for; he only knew it would be here soon. "I try not to worry too much, though. If it happens, it happens."

"I'll do the shopping again tomorrow if you like. Is there anything special you need?"

Buster thought about this for a moment as if it were an especially tricky parable.

"Not really," he said again. "These days it's hard for me to think too much about what I'll need tomorrow."

The following morning the troops arrived like a benediction.

Having ascended a large rocky summit of ice, Buster stood alone above the village with shy and awful grace, watching the planes spill men in white Arctic uniforms from their shining steel bellies. White, seamed parachutes blossomed, and the storm paratroopers landed running, disengaging themselves from their deflating nylon envelopes with adroit little tugs and zips, pulling pistols from their holsters and releasing well-trained battle cries into the gray air.

Dazedly, in dribs and drabs, the penguins waddled from their homes, rubbing their sleepy eyes against the harsh glare of searchlights and flash grenades. They raised their flippers in the air even before they knew who they were surrendering to, or why. Just some force of nature, they suspected. Some part of the world they never knew they didn't belong to.

Within moments they were herded into wire compounds wearing nothing more than their pajamas and stocking caps. They never fired a shot in self-defense, or uttered a word in anger or reproach.

"It's not fair to blame it all on testosterone," a voice told Buster from out of nowhere. "Because it's not men against women, you know, or even human beings against animals. It's animals against animals, and *that's* the scary part. It's animals against themselves, trying to conquer the deepest assumptions of their own bodies."

The voice had arrived on the wings of a crisp morning breeze, whipping up clouds of frost and ice. Buster had been expecting something like this for weeks.

Buster watched the distant jeeps and tanks assemble in the tiny village. Workmen in orange parkas were hanging klieg lights from high wooden poles.

At this point, Buster thought, a real hero would be planning brave insurrections and mutinies.

"There's only so much you can do in a given situation," the voice behind him said. "All you can do is the best you can, that's all. You do the best you can and then try to be kind to yourself afterward."

Buster turned. The large black crow was perched on a leaning iron pole.

"What's a black crow like you doing at the South Pole?" Buster asked.

The black crow was watching soldiers form ranks in the village below.

"What do you *think* I'm doing? I'm freezing my pimply little butt off, that's what."

PART 3

ENDS OF THE EARTH

1

MANIFEST DESTINY

They passed through howling storms and frozen tempests. They passed through regions of dizzying whiteness. They passed through blizzards of static electricity and bluish showers of cosmic debris. They weren't even certain where they were going. They knew only that they couldn't turn back.

Eventually they reached a ramshackle trading outpost on the rim of the Kantchung Peninsula. The outpost was managed by a wiry, obstreperous otter named Dave.

"What can I do you boys for?" Dave asked, offering them a table by the glowing coal fire. "Tea, hot chocolate, road maps, lodging?"

"J-j-j-just a little wh-wh-while by the f-f-f-fire would be n-nice," Buster chattered. He was slapping the circulation back into his wings and stamping the crusty ice from his boots. "I'm t-t-too cold to th-think."

Dave wiped his hands on the hem of his dingy apron and eyed Charlie suspiciously.

"How about you, pal? You want to order something? Or you boys just being sociable?"

Charlie scowled at the bar menu and tossed it spinning across the splintery wooden table.

"One room," he told Dave succinctly. "One double bed, two continental breakfasts, and two packed lunches to go. And as for right this moment, *pal*, I'll have a large Jameson's, straight up."

Charlie was leaning across the table, matching Dave's unblinking stare with a pretty unblinking stare of his own. He nudged Buster an aside with his frosty wing.

"How about you? Some bottled spirits to warm up the old circulation?"

"I-I-I d-d-d-d-don't know, Ch-Ch-Ch-Charlie. I c-c-c-c-can't s-s-s-seem to m-m-make up my m-m-mind."

Charlie and Dave continued observing one another in a sort of ocular standoff. All around them the small, cluttered igloo smelled of urine, dead fish, and rotting vegetable matter.

"Make that *two* large Jameson's," Charlie told Dave without blinking. "And like I said—hold the goddamn ice."

DAVE'S TRADING POST did sparse but profitable business with the local community of voles and snow martens. The local rodents couldn't believe their luck, nudging and grinning at one another while Dave toted their latest diggings on a small Trojan brand free scale.

"Three ounces of gold," Dave said evenly. "That means, let's see here"—scratching reflectively at a lined yellow legal pad—"you've just bought yourself three spanking brand-new kernels of grain. So name your poison, buddy. You want it in rice, corn, wheat, or what?"

The rodents carried away their supplies wrapped in oily white butcher paper, tittering shamelessly.

"Just imagine that!" they congratulated one another outside. "Food for rocks! Who *ever* would have figured, huh?"

"Happy voles," Charlie muttered cynically after his third Jameson's. Buster had fallen asleep against the table and was snoring fitfully. "Happy happy voles."

Charlie enjoyed the brief, edgy silence his cynicism invoked. He felt the slow heat of steam building.

"You got a problem with that, buddy?" Dave was securing his latest capital influx behind a solid steel door. He pulled a Schlage lock into place and clenched it shut with an abrupt little snap. "It's called commerce, pal. It's called the exchange value negotiated through competitive free trade. The voles put away some winter provision and I put away some cash toward my impending early retirement—what's more fair than that? I'm planning to buy this tropical island, see. Somewhere in the South Pacific. Mainly 'cause I'm so bloody sick of the South Pole I could puke."

Charlie dug deep into his parka for one of the choice items he had nicked over the years from bedroom bureaus, jewelry shops, and street-corner vendors.

"How much you give me for this?" Charlie slapped it down succinctly like punctuation.

Dave came over with a small glimmering jeweler's glass screwed into his right eye. He turned Charlie's bright stone in the light and snicked his tongue a few times.

"Not bad," he said.

Charlie emptied his glass and set it up for another.

"Human beings have invaded the western rim and they're headed this way," Charlie told Dave and the Trading Post's variously distracted inhabitants—a few boozy voles, a fox with a bum leg, and a scuzzy looking Eskimo chick wrapped up in mossy caribou pelts and coffee-stained sackcloth. "They've got tanks, barbed wire, electrified fences, history books, foreign trade secretaries, corporate spokespersons, and a lot of dumb, well-intentioned military grunts just looking for adventure and a good time. They've imprisoned every penguin they can lay their hands on and are currently teaching them to operate snow plows and word-processing equipment. Pretty soon the penguins will be empowered by the world court. They'll be expected to pay their fair share to the IMF, and issued their own military fatigues and helicopters. Then these suitably authorized penguins will be sent off to acculturate the seals, and the seals will be sent off to acculturate the walruses, and so on and so forth, ad nauseam, etcetera. *Click click click*—I believe in Southeast Asia it was referred to as the domino effect."

Dave was brushing the bluish diamond against his cheek, as if he found it soothing to his chapped, flaky skin.

"Oh really?" he responded distantly. He was thinking about his island in the South Pacific, where he intended to build a beautiful resort hotel with five-star nouvelle cuisine dining and the latest in satellite-dish TV. "Human beings—and they're looking for a good time? Well, jeez." Dave thrummed his fingers against the bar's grainy surface. Ta-ta-ta-ta-*tum*.

After another reflective moment he added, "This could mean some serious business opportunities for our close personal friend, yours truly."

Buster dreamed of Sandy, Estelle, Whistling Pete, and Pete Jr. They were ascending a smooth snowy hill, pulling a wooden toboggan on a frazzled rope.

"Let's go back," Pete Jr. implored. "I'm ready to go home, Dad."

Buster exchanged a quick look with Sandy and Estelle. The girls were holding hands with strange familiarity, wearing gray dungarees and red flannel shirts.

"Let's just climb a little farther, okay?" Whistling Pete indicated a high, misty copse of trees with one wool-mittened flipper. "Let's continue a bit farther, and then we can all go home for brandy crumpets and hot tea . . ."

Buster awoke with a start in a cramped, musty room, his heart racing from the dreamed exertion. The air was close and humid, his mattress damp, lumpy, and inflexible. He tried to reposition his bristly pillow.

"Jesus Christ," Charlie said. "Watch out, willya? That's my neck."

"Sorry," Buster said. He sat up and reached for a glass of water from the wobbly bedside table. An amazed wind whistled outside.

Dressed before dawn they found their way hesitantly down the dark, leaning stairway. In the lobby the crippled fox was snoring in his sleep. A dim yellow candle glowed behind the bar, where Dave the Otter was figuring the night's totals on a pocket calculator.

"Good morning," Dave said cheerily. "And how did you fine fellows sleep last night?" Dave's attitude had improved significantly ever since Charlie presented him the bluish diamond.

"Two black coffees," Charlie said. "And keep them coming."

They chewed dense, croissant-shaped pastries and drank their coffee at the wooden table. Beside them in the dark, the Eskimo chick was untangling a knotty mass of five-pound test fishing line in her lap, spinning it neatly around a small gray cardboard tube. The whites of her eyes gazed out at them from her grungy, tangled hair and sweat-stained animal pelts.

The Eskimo smiled, revealing stubby yellow teeth.

"Come here and I'll give you a tumble, Little Black One," she said, and patted her right thigh with a sealskin mitten. "Won't charge nothing, neither. That's 'cause I like you." She uttered the words with a mechanical incomplexity. It was like watching cans of peas roll off an assembly line.

Charlie refused to acknowledge anything but his black coffee. Within moments Buster watched the amorous invitation begin to shift his way.

"Hey, I mean, thanks anyway," Buster said. "But like, I been through a lot lately, and, well. I guess I'm just not into sex anymore. You mind?"

The Eskimo chick straightened her pelts and resumed spooling her tangly fishing line. She wiped her greasy forehead against the back of her hairy forearm.

"You're heading in wrong direction, bird brains," she said simply, gesturing at the white vistas. "Out where you're going, no furniture. No restaurants or gas stations. No newspapers, no governments, no suburbs, no clocks. Minds come untethered in places like that. Take it from me, birds. My name is Muk Luk and I know."

Dave the Otter helped them into their parkas, snowshoes, and hats. He strapped nylon backpacks over their shoulders and loaded them up with bagged lunches and provisions, two bottles of dubiously sealed Jameson's, three cans of Sterno, and a box of Blue Point matches.

"You come back soon now, y'hear?" Dave said, slapping the mud from their shoulders. "Remember—Dave's Outpost is *always* open."

Muk Luk was outside unloading a large, prehistoric-looking fish from her sled. The fish featured gnarly, crooked teeth, translucent whiskers, and weird dorsal extremities like tiny clenched fists.

"Big dinner," Muk Luk said proudly. "Mighty good protein

feast for me and any friends who might care to join me."

Charlie marched past her with a little swagger.

"Cheerio," Charlie said.

The departed storm had left the sky scrubbed with brightness. Pale glacial shapes rimmed the horizon. Without another word, Charlie and Buster proceeded into the trackless waste.

"I warned you about the tundra, no kidding," Muk Luk called out, following along in a rattly sled pulled by an anxious, unwormed husky named Rick. "Terrible forces lurk out there, forces even sneakier than our friend Dave the Otter. Very *nook-nook*, these spirits, very devious. In the regions of colorless ice, your warm animal flesh will not be without its admirers."

"Thanks for the warning, Muk Luk," Charlie called out briskly over his shoulder. "Don't forget to write."

"May the great white spirit protect you from all the nasty little spirits running around," Muk Luk said. She brought her sled to a halt, pots and pans dully chiming, and performed a concise genuflection.

"Take care of yourself, Black One," she added in a whisper. "Muk Luk thinks you're kind of cute."

Charlie's heels stirred up clouds of frost that stung Buster's eyes and cheeks. All around them the landscape lacked weather and definition.

"By the way, Charlie," Buster interposed. "Where *are* we going, anyway? I don't mean to keep pestering you, but it's something I'd like to know."

"It's not where we're going that matters," Charlie said. "It's what we're leaving behind." Charlie gestured at the past's dim horizon, where the figures of Muk Luk, her dog, and her sled had diminished to brief, shimmering ellipses.

Muk Luk waved good-bye one last time.

"L'amant de neige," she muttered bitterly. Wiping a crusty tear

from one eye, she watched the small birds disappear into the vast staticky whiteness.

Then Muk Luk turned her mangy sled around and went home.

"So this is the part that confuses me, Charlie," Buster said, skidding across the crusty powder in his oversized pink snowshoes. "If we want to warn everybody the humans are coming, then why're we heading off where there ain't nobody around to warn? I mean, Dave's Trading Post isn't exactly Boston, Massachusetts, you know."

"It's perfectly simple," Charlie said, trudging ahead with dogged consistency, as if he were stamping out counterfeit coins with his feet. "I'm an animal-rights activist, committed to furthering the cause of my animal brethren throughout the universe. But at the same time, see, I also *really* need to be alone."

Every so often a steel gray military jet passed overhead, pulling behind it a taut pink ribbon of exhaust. Whenever one of these jets appeared, Buster and Charlie would huddle underneath their white camouflage blanket, nibbling fugitively at thin butter sandwiches and chocolatey digestive biscuits.

Charlie gestured with the crust of his Wonder Bread.

"That's a Mirage F1CR-200 spy plane, Buster. It's got a twenty-seven-foot wingspan, an in-flight refueling boom, infrared cameras, and a complete range of airmobile image-processing equipment. That sucker can outfly, outsee, and outbattle any animal that was ever conceived of in the history of this feeble Animal Planet. I may not care much for human beings, Buster, but you gotta hand them one thing. They sure do some crazy things with metal."

They journeyed into regions of white storm and cold conquest where they encountered primitive cultures and strange, savage

48

dialects even Charlie couldn't entirely comprehend. A wandering tribe of shaggy polar bears wearing wolf-head masks, bone necklaces, and burred, mossy dreadlocks who worshiped a rudely claw-carved wooden totem named Awe. A paranoid community of mollusks who could speak only two words and accomplish two purposes: "Procreate!" and "Die!" A couple of foxes with bad skin, a half-mad sea tortoise trying to mate with an aluminum pie tin, and a lone albatross drowsing in the branches of a dead tree.

"They call themselves human beings," Charlie tried to warn them, resorting to rough wing gestures and ice-scrawled rebuses when he had to. "They've got two legs, two hands, two eyes, and two ears. They walk on these big thick feet they've developed, kind of like me, see, only with these long arms swinging at their sides. They can't swim very well without a lot of overpriced technical equipment; they can't fly, they can't smell, and they're ugly as mortal sin. But just because they're ugly and kind of stupid, whatever you do, *don't* underestimate them. Okay, troops, repeat after me: *Hu*-man *Be*-ings. I'll say it again. *Hu*-man *Be*-ings. Okay, now. *Everybody!*"

The pack of wary echinoderms glanced around self-consciously. They held their spears and shields with a loose-limbed discomposure.

"Ho-hum beanies," they muttered in a weak, ragged chorus, shuffling anxiously from side to side. *"Ho*-hum *bean*-ies."

"No no no, you blithering spelunkers! How are you going to combat a menace you can't even pronounce? Now come *on*— and I mean *everybody*. Let me *hear* you!"

Everywhere they traveled, Charlie wielded his fiercest and most inspired oratory, causing many highly placed savages to fear his conviction. Village elders and witch doctors shook shrunken heads at Charlie, or tried to dispel his pungent rhetoric with burning incense and smoky torches. They claimed Charlie and Buster were evil spirits, bad Gods, figments of illusion, terrible dreams unleashed in the night.

"Big fish in small ponds," Charlie explained to his slowly blinking acolytes and hangers-on. "They want to keep you stupid so they can continue seeming wise. If they've got such heapum big medicine, why do they want our heads on a platter, huh? I'll tell you why, you jabbering primordial boneheads. It's because the imminent human oppression I'm warning you about is the same age-old oppression your local politicos have been practicing on you for generations. Remember this, guys—Charlie's First Law. It's not man against animal, or male against female, or even proles against bourgeoisie. It's *us* against *them.*"

Night after night they were roused from their sleep and urged into scratchy clothing while swift offerings of doughy flour and salted meat were shoved into their pockets. Then they fled through the darkness pursued by hooded animals with flickering torches and wild baying wolves on long leather leashes.

"Holy mackerel, Charlie," Buster complained during the most strenuous periods of fleeing, his blubber flapping against itself with the sound of wet laundry in a sirocco. "I heard something about they want to feed us our own bowels on a stick. It's called the ogle-crunch ceremony or something."

"The Ogle and Munch," Charlie corrected, and pulled Buster into the abrupt, frosty aperture of a cavernous passageway.

"Ow ow ow, Charlie!" Buster was wriggling and squealing. The front half of his body was plunged in darkness, his buns and toes upended and exposed to the rushing, malevolent white world. "Help me, I'm stuck!"

"Come on, Buster. Quit fooling around." Charlie fastened onto Buster's bristling lapels and, taking a determined breath, *pulled.*

"Ow ow ow, Charlie, I mean it—I'm *stuck!*"

"You're not stuck, bun brain. You're too tense. Now take a deep breath and try to *relax*."

"Relax, Charlie? You want me to *relax!*"

Fear had dilated Buster's pupils until he could see the long, moody cavern, gnarly with stalagmites. Behind them in the dark the mob of howling black boars came thundering closer, their blazing torches upraised like murderous clubs.

"All intruders must die!" they screamed. *"Especially* the penguin!"

Buster took a hard deep breath, clenched shut his eyes, and felt his bowels evacuate with a splash.

At the exact same moment, Charlie grabbed Buster by the neck and gave him a terrific yank—and with a wet, soggy plop Buster landed in the refrigerated cavern just as the scrabbling boars roared past overhead.

"Close call," Charlie said, falling back against Buster's panting stomach with a sigh.

Bright, refracted starlight whirled in the cavern like illuminated insects. Buster could smell the sharp, acidic tang of his own incontinence staining the snow outside.

"Tell me about it," Buster said.

2

BAD LOVE

Back at Dave's Trading Post, Muk Luk pined and fretted away her days in a perilously leaning, Welfare-subsidized igloo constructed from ice, wire mesh, and Styrofoam packing insulation. The only Eskimo of her tribe to be relocated to the South Pole by America's Federal Housing Program (which had decided to save money by offering housing to needy people in places they didn't want to live), Muk Luk had eventually subsided into this strange new world with all her oldest, most familiar feelings of loneliness and anomie. In fact, some mornings she was so depressed she couldn't even get out of bed to go to the bathroom to brush her teeth. She just lay there for hours, chewing beef jerky and examining herself in a small handheld mirror encrusted with grimy costume jewelry.

"No matter how much you tart yourself up, and no matter how many budget cosmetics you order through your local Avon representative, you will never be attractive by any means," Muk Luk informed her puffy reflection. "No matter how politely you behave, nor how generously you offer your bodily fluids to strangers, human men will never do anything but disdain you, even sexually repressed military personnel, such as those you've occasionally bonked at the local weather stations. In fact, if it weren't for large doses of Dave's whiskey carefully applied, you probably wouldn't engage in *any* sexual activity whatsoever. And when you come right down to it, what good is a heavily sedated man, anyway? Well, maybe a little more good than the various slimy pseudomammals you've been known to bring home. Maybe a little more good than the tattered dirty magazines you recover from military trash bins, or the long-distance call-in sex lines you desperately engage through pay phones, or the gas-powered vibrators you purchase from dubious mail-order catalogs."

Gazing into her handheld vanity mirror, Muk Luk felt the terrible absence in her heart and she cried. Everything Muk Luk desired was negated by these hairy, heavily pockmarked cheeks, calamitous teeth, and red, rheumy eyes.

There were small rewards in her life, but not many. The resident heat of Rick the Husky's body in her bed, and the thin blanket of soft blond hairs he was perpetually shedding throughout the cluttered apartment like dingy manna. There was the flickering illumination of Dave's Trading Post on the hill, and the occasional choice cigarette butt discarded from roving military helicopters. Some nights, emboldened by cheap alcohol, Muk Luk even enjoyed a minor epiphany of sorts, staggering to the summit of a nearby snowy dune and gazing up at the radiant amazement of auroras and stars. A universe ruled by light, swirling with physics and indeterminacy. Distant, incomprehensible planets inhabited by strange bugs, birds, flowers, elephants, and trees. Submarine creatures, creatures that subsisted on plutonium and silicon, creatures without mouths or eyes or minds to make things matter. Lying on her back against the impacted ice, Muk Luk wondered at the bright universe and relapsed into her slow, swelling discontent. Stars popped and plummeted out there. Others exploded and collapsed. The universe wasn't much more than a violent altercation, really, an infinitude of biological accidents and catastrophes. If you looked far away from the inhospitality of your own body, life ceased to mean anything. There was just all that light, all that motion, all that space you didn't belong to.

If you thought about the universe in all its breadth and complexity, then logically your own sadness shouldn't matter. But the crazy thing was, your own sadness always did.

One morning during winter's waning Muk Luk was unloading supplies from her sled when she heard a thin mechanical revving in the distance. The tearing sound kept flat to the horizon, churning up a long plume of icy exhaust in its wake.

In the doorway of Muk Luk's igloo, Rick the Husky wagged his ever-optimistic tail and grinned.

"Company's coming," Rick said. "What do you think of the chances, Muk Luk? You might even get laid."

The jeep was army issue, and the two men in it wore shaggy white wool parkas, matching trousers, and wide tinted sunglasses. Their faces were weather roughened and raw.

"Lieutenant Jack Hollister, ma'am," the driver said. "Navy Intelligence." The jeep continued revving, as if anxious to get somewhere. "And this is my Soviet liaison, Sergeant Yuri Rudityev."

Hollister performed a curt, patronizing salute while Yuri sneered around at the filthy reservation. The modular-style tract of crumbling, abandoned igloos. Overturned trash barrels and rusty steel sleds. The smell of animal urine and spoiled whale blubber.

"What a bloody tip, wankers." Yuri had spent the last few months attached to a cultural-exchange unit in East London, and he still loved to exert the warm round shape of foreign vowels in his mouth. "Flippin' 'eck. Get a load of this grungy squat."

Lieutenant Hollister removed an eight-by-ten glossy photograph from his pouch pocket. He handed it to Muk Luk and instantly she knew. It was the message she had been waiting for all her life, passing through her skin like a thin field of electricity.

"You ever see this joker around?" Hollister asked. He propped his sunglasses on his forehead, giving Muk Luk the full benefit of his suspicious peer. "We think maybe he's traveling in the company of a small black-and-white penguin."

Muk Luk held the photograph in both hands like a psalm. If she had a beautiful voice, she could sing it. Then the entire world would know.

"We don't want to hurt them," Hollister said. "We only want to help them understand."

Muk Luk looked at the photo one more time. Then, in her warmly blossoming heart, she said good-bye, and surrendered it with all the noble indifference she could muster.

"Stranger to me, stranger," Muk Luk told the Lieutenant.

And began reloading the provisions onto her sled.

"Seen these guys?" echoed Dave the Otter. "Hell, I wish I never. But I'm a compassionate sort of guy, right? A couple of my fellow animals show up out here, hungry and cold, well, I make them at home. I give them warm beds to sleep in. I listen to their sob stories. That's what the world's all about, ain't it? The Judeo-Christian heritage and all that?"

Lieutenant Hollister cleared his throat, removing a dull pencil and a blue loose-leaf notebook from his shirt pocket. Sergeant Rudityev was busily pouring himself another tall glass of Stolichnaya.

"Cheers, you stupid tossers," Yuri told the bar's smelly disreputables, and showed them his tall glass before perfunctorily draining it.

Outside in the faintly falling, falling faintly snow, Muk Luk leaned into the frosty window, breaking the cold glare with her furry mittens. Dead fish were smoking on a wire rack over the fireplace, and a group of wary voles were being lured into a crooked card game by a pair of traveling corn-liquor salesmen.

"Subversive literature, *that's* what they were selling," Dave told the Lieutenant, pouring himself and the officers more free booze as he swelled with self-importance. "I never actually *seen* any of it, right, but it's pretty obvious, ain't it? They show up out here ratty and half-starved. They don't mix socially with the other guests. They keep to themselves and don't even join in with any of the gambling or whoring. All they do is act better than everybody else and spout off a lot of highly *political* mumbo jumbo. Denigrating you fine military types. Talking about animal oppression and the 'so-called' free market. We've heard it all a million times before, haven't we? A lot of subversive chatter that never did any animals any good, just stirred up a whole lot of pointless blood and struggle. Look at you Russian guys, right? You finally learned the errors of *your* ways, didn't you?"

Yuri didn't respond, by this point immobilized by vodka. He stared into his empty glass as if he were explicating chemistry through a microscope.

"Pointless blood," Yuri said softly, with a drunkard's meaningless clarity. "Pointless struggle."

Outside in the snow, Muk Luk and Rick the Husky heard the incoming night sweep toward them across the white ice like a manta ray, accompanied by a sparkling flutter of ionized particles. Muk Luk felt the hard *click* of temperature in the frosty window. Rick paced in a tight circle two or three times to get warm.

"Let's either go after them," Rick grumbled irritably, "or get back to bed."

But of course by this point Muk Luk had already decided.

She made sure the doors and windows of her igloo were double-locked and bolted, that the Sterno was extinguished, and the radio turned off. Then she wrapped herself in the layered stain and muddle of her entire furry wardrobe, and ate everything in her refrigerator not fit to carry.

Minutes later she was driving Rick the Husky across the spuming snow.

"I much prefer action to self-pity," Rick confessed, thrilling to the rise of his own heat and adrenalin. "I mean, making the *effort* is a lot more important than getting good results, don't you think? But on the other hand, I'll sure miss our toasty bed."

They were flying across the white world on skimming steel runners. They were hurtling into the quickening future rather than dreading the inviolate past.

56

"There are better things worth living for than our own hurt and misery," Muk Luk declared to the white permafrost. "There are better things worth dying for, too."

3

A DISCOURSE ON NATURE

"Nasty, brutish, and short," Lieutenant Hollister proclaimed, popping a Pall Mall between his lips. "That's what Thomas Hobbes had to say about nature, Yuri, and nobody ever said it better. Nature red in tooth and claw. A vast hairy malaise of poisonous bugs, hissing snakes, rabid squirrels, and rocky beds. You look at nature, Yuri, and what do you see? Urine and feces everywhere. Rotting corpses and maggoty meat. You know what nature's composed of, once you journey outside the warm, protective environs of our cities, shopping centers, and public schools? It's a big toilet bowl, that's what nature is. A big bloody cannibal feast. Everybody eating everybody else. Shitting everywhere and chewing up the scenery. So don't try giving me any of that communistical 'Oh how I love Mother Nature' crap, Yuri. Because I just don't buy it."

They were driving back to the new military base on Penguin Island while Yuri leaned his forehead against the padded dash, moaning in a distressful self-communion. "Oh Mummy," Yuri drooled. "What a royal pisser." Yuri had spent all last night drinking vodka and all that morning throwing up.

"You know what I think we should do to Mother Nature, Yuri? I think we should tie her down with ropes. I think we should beat her over the head with a big stick. I think we should lock her in an iron cage with a television, some stuffed chairs, and a case of Diet Pepsi. And if Mother Nature makes a fuss? We hose her down with cold water and cut off her chow line. Because Mother Nature needs to learn *discipline,* Yuri. She needs a solid tour of duty with the good old-fashioned U.S. Marines."

Penguin Island was connected to the mainland by a short pontoon bridge erected by the first armored division. New tar and gravel roads had been laid, telephone lines established, and various corporate franchises installed. McDonald's. Burger King. Pizza Hut. Safeway. Wal-Mart and Unocal. The canning factory had been shut down and replaced by a gigantic Bob's Discount Warehouse. These days, local penguins either worked as "food-dispensers" for one of the corporate franchises or as junior clerks at the new military base.

"I love Burger King," Yuri said, with a faint gleam in his eye. Then, as succinct as a genuflection, he leaned over the side of the jeep and retched up the last few drops of green bile his roiling stomach possessed.

"You know who started all this 'love nature' crap, don't you, Yuri?" Hollister had pulled the jeep up to the new Military HQ, which was conveniently located next door to what was formerly the Ice Floe Bar & Grill, and what was presently the Officer's Mess. "Jean Jacques Rousseau, that's who. Another one of you flaky Europeans, Yuri, and please don't take that personal or anything. Have you ever read Jean Jacques Rousseau, Yuri? My motto's always been 'Get to know the enemy before the enemy gets to know you.'"

Hollister cranked on the emergency brake and leapt out of the jeep. He was already unzipping his shaggy white overcoat when he came around to help Yuri disboard.

"Oh, Jesus Christ, matey," Hollister said. He was looking at the mess Yuri had made down the side of their freshly requisitioned army jeep. "This is what I call goddamn unprofessional."

"Jean Jacques Rousseau was the first communistical type to talk about communal living, and peaceful coexistence, and nuclear disarmament, and God knows what else. He had this crazy idea that nature is a wonderful place. Go back to nature, he kept saying. Be *one* with glorious Mother Nature. Kiss the earth, fuck an Indian, marry a tree. Jean Jacques Rousseau, incidentally, was a self-confessed masturbator, liar, thief, and perhaps even a homosexual. God, sometimes I don't know who I hate most. The goddamn Communists or the goddamn homosexuals. It's so, I don't know. So *natural,* I guess. So steeped in the vile squalor of nature, all the awful pain and imprecision of it. Butt fucking, Yuri. That's what's ruining this great world of ours. A bunch of retarded animal types who can't tell one hole from another."

Lieutenant Hollister was smoking his Pall Mall and being blithely carried along by the warm integrity of his own voice. He heard Yuri snoring faintly beside him in the brightly lacquered, harshly fluorescent waiting room. It felt so good, Lieutenant Hollister thought. It felt so good to finally understand what the world of nature was all about.

"The General will see you now."

Lieutenant Hollister glanced up. The receptionist didn't look half bad for her age. She was wearing a misty haze of blush and cosmetics, and a tight lacy skirt that showed off her spectacularly large, wobbly behind.

Lieutenant Hollister loved girls with big behinds. Especially native girls.

"Thank you, dear," Hollister said, reaching out to give slumbering Yuri a little stir. He felt a sparkle of confidence rise up from his chest. It was like inhaling bubbles off the surface of a glass of champagne.

Then, suddenly, his newfound confidence was speaking itself on his lips.

"And what might your name be, honey?"

The penguin looked at him out of one cocked, disamusing eyeball.

"My name's Sandy, Officer. And I might as well let you know right now. I'm already married."

General Heathcliff was in a jovial mood. Promoted just two weeks before, he had been flown in from London after distinguishing himself as Head Caretaker in charge of the London Zoo Rationalization Program. Now he had a higher rank, better pay, and his pick of the local native girls. As a result, General Heathcliff was very, very happy. He didn't even mind Antarctica that much.

"These are good people," General Heathcliff generously pronounced, passing around a bowl of mixed nuts. "These are kind people. These are simple people. You know what your average penguin wants out of life, boys? A nice evening meal of greens and mackerel. A warm place to go to the bathroom. And maybe a little raw nookie out behind the snowplow. Penguins don't run themselves ragged with a lot of big, overpriced ambitions like us humans do. Fancy automobiles, say, or luxury yachts. That's because penguins experience the fullness of life in ways us corrupted Homo sapiens types never will. I don't want to spoil that for them, understand? When I leave Penguin Island in a year or two, I want to think I'm leaving these penguins just as sweet and innocent as the day I found them. Do you boys follow me? Do you have any idea how much more important the *quality* of life is than the *quantity?*"

"Absolutely, sir. My thoughts exactly."

Hollister suppressed a deep, labyrinthine yawn, one that reached up from his belly and his toes. Yuri had fallen asleep again and was faintly snoring against Hollister's left shoulder insignia.

The General droned on and on, making the neat, featureless office seem increasingly remote and inspecific.

"A little knowledge is a dangerous thing, and that's what I want to protect these cute little penguins from. Knowledge, boys. A lot of intellectual mumbo jumbo that'll just worry their puny little brains." The General was gnawing a large, flaky brazil nut. He got up and came around his desk with an informal, self-deprecating shrug. "And I don't need to tell you that despite the remarkable progress we've made in the world of international diplomacy lately, there are still some pretty sneaky, evil creatures running around. Creatures who talk too much. Creatures who think they know all the answers. Creatures with bad attitudes toward authority. Creatures who don't believe in our free-market economy. I think you boys know precisely the sorts of creatures I'm talking about."

General Heathcliff perched on the corner of his varnished black desk. He was looking directly at an eight-by-ten glossy photograph tacked to a bulletin board on the bathroom door. The glossy photograph depicted the face of a large black crow. A shiny red bull's eye was painted over the crow's face with what looked like nail polish.

The General himself, however, wasn't looking at the glossy photograph. Instead, he was looking into Hollister's eyes and making sure *he* looked at it.

"Some men are called on by history, Hollister. These men are ordained by God, or by the World Spirit, or by the Great What-have-you. These men must be ready to make the Big Decisions."

"I realize that, sir."

"Are you one of those men, Hollister? Are *you* ready to make the Big Decisions when called upon by History?"

"I hope so, sir."

"Do you believe in your country, Hollister? Do you believe in all the little countries, like poor Yuri's there, that need us around to protect and inspire them? Little countries *want* to be good, Hollister. They *want* to be like us. But at the same time, they need our shining example to point them the way. Especially these days, Hollister. When sometimes the night gets so black you can hardly see your own hand in front of your face."

"I know what I have to do, and I'm fully capable of doing it, sir."

Yuri continued to slumber, breathing fitfully into Hollister's left ear. In many ways, this was the happiest moment of Lieutenant Hollister's entire life.

The General performed a curt little shrug and clasped his hands together in his lap, as if he were cradling a scared baby bird in the mesh of his fingers.

"So tell me, son. Tell me what you'll need."

Hollister was looking at the half-depleted can of Planter's Mixed Nuts on the General's desk. He imagined that every individual nut was a hand grenade, and that every hand grenade contained a tiny metal pin.

He spoke with a conviction and self-confidence he had never felt before.

"I need a Sikorsky EH-60C Blackhawk, sir. I need it fitted with a GR-9 intercept receiver and a TLQ-27A jammer. I need the full range of Aircraft Survivability Equipment, and flare dispensers mounted in the tailboom. I need flak jackets. I need Code R Clearance. I need a brilliant tail gunner, like Yuri here, and heat-seeking missiles, and a grenade launcher, sir. I need it all by tomorrow at oh-six-hundred hours, sir, and then I promise. Our big-mouthed friend mounted on the bathroom door?"

"Yes, Hollister?"

This time it was Hollister's turn to gesture, and the General's turn to look.

"Just give me one week, sir," Hollister said. "And I'll blow that cheeky little bastard right out of the sky."

4

THE UTOPIAN IMPULSE

Some nights Buster lay awake beside the crackling fire and tried to remember what his life had been like before Charlie. Back then, when life had seemed so unreal, he awoke every morning before six to take out the trash. Then he fired up the wood stove and activated the gas central heating. By the time he finished his ablutions, Sandy was already poaching his eggs and frying his toast. Then they went off to their respective jobs, came home, listened to the radio, and went back to bed. Much like the island on which he was born, Buster's life had been perfectly circumscribed by routine and nonadventure. Sometimes Buster missed his old life and wanted it back. Other times, though, it all seemed terribly detached and meaningless, like photographs and memorabilia snatched from somebody's else's scrapbook.

"Charlie?"

"Hmm?"

"When it's all over, where will you go?"

Charlie rolled over in his ragged muddle of pelts and plastic tarpaulins. "What do you mean where will I go?"

"I mean where will you *go*, Charlie? You don't want to spend the rest of your life out here, do you? In *Antarctica?*"

Logs cracked and disassembled. The red heart of the fire

glowed momentarily brighter and a strange softness fell over the minimal encampment. Something unfamiliar was happening, Buster thought. It was almost like being *relaxed*.

After a while Charlie said, "I guess if I could be anywhere I wanted, I'd probably go live in the country, like maybe New England or the South of France. Some place with seasons in it. Fall, winter, summer, you know. And I'd stay put for good this time, no more migratory hassles for me ever again, all that ridiculous packing and unpacking and storing things in everybody's basement. I've done my share of traveling, Buster. I've done my share of searching for greener pastures. When I finally settle down, boy, I intend to really *settle down*."

Buster rolled onto one elbow and tried to look into Charlie's eyes, but Charlie's eyes were closed. Charlie's back was to the fire, his face as black and featureless as a silhouette.

"Would you have a house, Charlie? If you were going to live somewhere all year round, you'd need a house, wouldn't you? Would you have a guest room, Charlie? I mean, if I were to come and visit, would there be a place for me?"

"I'd have tiers and tiers of guest rooms, Buster, don't you worry. It'd be a house with enough space to accommodate dozens, perhaps even hundreds of visitors, friends, and extended-family members, free keys and electric blankets for everybody. If you're like a snow marten, or a cardinal, or even a peripatetic penguin such as yourself, Buster, and you happen to find yourself in my neck of the woods? Well, you'd be goddamn welcome anytime of the year, no kidding. A place where everybody takes what they need and gives what they can afford."

"What about food, Charlie? What about curtains and furniture?"

"A couple of enormous refrigerator-freezers, packed with goodies. Häagen-Dazs, Buster. Corn dogs, chili con carne, Sarah Lee Pound Cake, all the Pringles you can eat. And no drapes or curtains at all, because we'd have nothing to be ashamed of, right? Certainly not our sexuality, or our bodily functions, or our bad moods and blemishes. We'd just let the whole wide world stare in at us, Buster. What would we care?"

"We wouldn't care at all, would we, Charlie?" Buster was breathing a little faster. "And because we'd be taking care of each other, we wouldn't have to worry about anything, right? About Army Intelligence, or kids with BB guns, or, I hate to say it, but *you know*, Charlie. We wouldn't even have to worry about *them*."

"Cats," Charlie concluded emphatically. He sounded as calm and disaffected as a math teacher announcing the solution of a logarithm. "We wouldn't have to worry about *anything*, Buster, especially not cats. We'd be what they call a self-sustaining, self-governing, self-determining community. Which means we wouldn't just sit around waiting for some human being or religious charismatic to come along and make our decisions for us. We'd simply *be ourselves*, probably for the first time in our natural lives. If somebody didn't like the way we acted, or the way we chose to live, well, they could just *leave*. No hard feelings. We'd show them straight to the door."

It was the best night's sleep either of them had enjoyed in ages. When they awoke the next morning, the campfire was extinguished and warm spring sunlight was pouring down out of the blue sky. All across the permafrost Buster could hear the bright, brittle sounds of ice cracking.

They gathered up their few possessions with a new affection, like wondrous religious artifacts or letters from home. Two plastic spoons, two forks. Two battered aluminum plates and one iron saucepan. A large packet of beef jerky and a smaller packet of Bull Durham smoking tobacco. It wasn't as if life was more fully lived out here in the wilderness, Buster thought. It was just more easily accounted for.

The two set out with a renewed sense of purpose. For the first time in their travels, they weren't in a hurry to *get* somewhere, or to get *away* from somewhere else.

"Wouldn't it be great, Charlie, if like there really *was* this worldwide animal revolution and all?" Buster was a leaner, hungrier version of himself, with firm haunches and a grizzly, unshaven face. He had learned there was just no telling how far a penguin could walk if he set his mind to it. "Animals living together in perfect harmony, like this amazing leap forward in terrestrial evolution. Not a group mind or anything simple like that, Charlie, but just this really benevolent animal *concord,* like music, Charlie, only sweeter and more lasting. Animals helping each other get by. Horses, dogs, birds, beasts, humans beings, gorillas, shrimp, perch, zebras, and giraffes. Roaming freely all over the world. Sharing their thoughts and opinions, their food and their beds. Wouldn't that be great, Charlie? Wouldn't *that* be really *something?*"

"Absolutely," Charlie said. He was marching with a lighter step than ever before, showing Buster the way. "I couldn't have said it any better myself."

It was a great moment, Buster thought, a single point in time when they didn't need anything but dreams to sustain them. Wouldn't it be great? Wouldn't it be great if this moment could last forever?

But of course it couldn't last. Not even for another moment.

"What's that?"

"What's what, Charlie?"

A white instant. A faint whistle of wind and expectation.

"I don't hear anything, Charlie. What are you talking about?"

"That," Charlie said. He had swung his backpack onto the ground. *"That."*

Thin. Unresonant. Filled with flat spaces. Just a rhythm at first. A vague melody.

Duh-duh-*duh*, duh-duh-*duh*, duh-duh-*duh*.

"*That*, Charlie," Buster whispered. "What's *that?*"

'ere we go, duh-duh, *'ere* we go.

Charlie was already disentangling their white camouflage blanket from the backpack.

'ere we go, 'ere we go, 'ere we go!

"Footballers?" Charlie said, grimacing. "That's funny. I didn't think anybody in Antarctica even *played* football."

They saw it before they heard its muddy thunder, a black knobby shape sweeping toward them across the flat plains with faceted glass eyes like some prehistoric insect. A helicopter. An army-green whirring helicopter.

> *'ere we go,*
> > *'ere we go,*   'ERE WE GO!
> > *'ere we go,*

The voice was booming out across the plains through a pair of enormous Blaupunkt loudspeakers mounted on both sides of the nose like weirdly arched eyebrows. The roar of the engine was overtaking the helicopter itself, and then suddenly the wind whipping past, ruffling their feathers with a hot dry belligerence, like bullies pushing past on a subway.

"But, Charlie," Buster said. He was staring at the miraculous leering speed of it. The *fit-fit-fit* of the rotors seemed at once compelling and profound. "What's a helicopter looking for way out *here?*"

At this point Charlie pulled the white camouflage blanket up over their heads with a flourish. It *whoofed* open like a parachute and settled over them like a shroud.

"Who the hell do you *think* they're looking for, Buster?"

Fear was cold and mechanical, Buster thought, not feverish and clammy like you'd expect.

Then the thunder was lifting up from the ice and rock, rattling at their camouflage blanket. They heard nothing and they heard everything and then they heard nothing again and the shadow of the machine roared over them like a miniature storm and diminished again into the blue sky.

'ere we go, **duh-duh-duh,** *'ere we go.*

Duh-duh-*duh*, duh-duh-duh, *duh*-duh-duh.

The air was cold again.

The sun turned from yellow to white.

After a few more invisible beats, Buster took a deep breath.

And started to his feet.

"Jesus, Charlie. That was a close call—"

But he didn't see the same relief in Charlie's eyes. Instead, Charlie stood poised on the verge of his own attention, peering into the helicopter's ebbing thunder with an abstract scowl.

"Listen," he whispered. "Just *listen.*"

Buster saw the shadow first, rippling on the horizon.

And then the rotors.

And then the voice of it.

Duh-duh-*duh*, duh-duh-duh, *duh*-duh-duh.

"They've picked us up on infrared," Charlie said, as matter-of-fact as a bus announcer sending passengers to gate 27. "We're gonna have to run for it."

Headquarters refused them the Sikorsky, but finally came through with a Bell AH-1 Cobra, which featured a General Electric turret under nose with a M197 20mm. three-barrel gun, and a Minigun plus 40mm. grenade-launcher.

"The Sikorsky's a bit overkill, don't you think?" suggested the General. "After all—we're only talking about a couple of stupid birds."

The Cobra lacked the sort of high-tech sophistication that usually sent Hollister's hormones spinning. But he liked riding high in the cockpit, with wild boyish Yuri in full view below him, furiously manning the weaponry and microphones.

"We've got the little bastards now," Hollister said. He was taking the 'copter around in a keen 360-degree pivot. "I think it's time we cooked ourselves a little bird pudding."

Then he drove the Cobra down toward the white ice until there was nowhere the fleeing birds could run but up.

It wasn't like fear at all. It was like turning on an appliance, or activating some secret interior engine in yourself. It was like life, really. Like some perfect implicit expression of life itself.

"Run, Buster! To the top of the hill! Run like you've never run before!"

Buster was already trying, the slushy ice absorbing his energy like a sponge. It was like running up a down escalator. It was like running in a dream.

"Up the hill and over!" Charlie shouted. He was behind Buster, pushing at his buttocks with both wings. "You can do it, Buster! I know you can!"

The bullets were hitting the snow with muffled, splattery pops. *Plup-pluppa-plup.* It was almost funny, the sound the bullets made. Buster almost laughed.

The helicopter gliding down through the air like a summons, drawing the moment thin and resonant. You could hear every sound your own blood made. You could hear every whisper.

"You gotta believe, Buster, even when it doesn't make sense! You gotta believe there's something over that hill, something worth running for, some place you've always dreamed of getting to. Perfect community, Buster. Eternal love, great sex, loads of cash, I don't care, Buster. Anything, *anything at all.* But whatever you do, run faster than those bullets. Run faster than that overpriced machinery coming at us. Run faster than time, Buster, because that's what it means, see? When you're running toward something you believe in, you're running outside history itself. You're running toward places only your mind can get to. *Believe,* Buster. *Believe* that a better world's waiting for us on the other side of that hill!"

Buster felt the lean hard-knotted muscles in his calves and his flanks. He was strong. He was hungry. He was all-penguin.

"A few more yards, Buster. And then dive, no matter what's out there. No matter what's waiting for us—just *DIVE!*"

Plup-plup-pluppa-pluppa-plup-plup.

The bright blue sky. The startling white ice. And then the round summit, the verge of all possibility. Altitude, oxygen, atmosphere, light.

They felt the heat and wind of the rotors on their backs as they reached the summit and then they were looking down into the face of it. Perfect love. Total happiness. The ideal utopian world, waiting for them with open arms.

"It's you," Buster whispered, hurling himself over the summit, his soft round body floating through the air like a blind dirigible. "I never thought it would be you."

She was standing on the brow of the hill, wrapped in muddled furs. The biggest, ugliest, and most wonderful-looking female Eskimo anybody had ever seen in the entire history of the Animal Planet.

And she was poised to hurl an enormous metal spear.

5

ON TARGET

The white ice rushed to greet Buster as he splashed and tumbled in a confused assortment of limbs and expectations.

Charlie was next over the hill, the helicopter's vast shadow wrapping itself around him. Then, from out of nowhere, Charlie felt Muk Luk's hard hand on his shoulder, pushing him out of the way.

"Watch out," Rick the Husky warned from where he lay in back of the barricaded sled. "And let the lady do what the lady does best."

Then Muk Luk was taking four long striding steps across the ice, arched, wristy, tiptoed, and sublime. Everything about her for these few moments was totally perfect.

"Maybe she's not half so ugly as I thought," Buster conceded, and lapsed exhausted into the unconscious snow.

The helicopter lifted over the summit of the hill like a dull green God, wrathful and indolent, rotors churning, guns blazing away.

Then the spear was in the air.

And Charlie watched.

There was a crack and a chatter and the spear penetrated the whirring rotors, pinning the entire helicopter to the blue sky like a butterfly specimen to a killing tray.

The rotors missed a beat. Two beats. Three.

'ere we go
    'ere we go—

Then the entire machine performed an extraordinary backflip.

Then, just in case nobody had been watching the first time, it performed another.

"Muk Luk hate the military-industrial complex," Muk Luk said, shrugging her stiff shoulders. "Muk Luk wish they take all their stupid toys and go home."

The helicopter landed upside down in the snow with a lumbering crack. There was a slow pause like an afterthought.

Then, succinctly, it exploded.

Drifts of glass and metal fluttered over the breathless spectators like snowflakes at Christmas. Muk Luk and Charlie took two steps to the hill's summit and gazed down.

"Jesus, Muk Luk," Charlie said. "I guess there's only one thing left to say."

Muk Luk's lips were pursed. Oily flames reflected in her eyes like a memory of determination.

"What's that, Black Bird?"

Charlie shrugged deferentially.

"Nice shot, lady."

PART 4

CULTURE-AT-LARGE

1

ANIMALS IMAGINE

Voices were carrying across the entire surface of the spinning Animal Planet.

"Charlie got away. They sent Air Force fucking-One after the bastard, and he got *away.*"

"I hear Charlie shot them out of the sky with a bazooka."

"A whole fleet of them—MIG fighters armed to the teeth with heat seekers and heavy artillery."

"He's armed?"

"And he's pissed off."

"And he's passing out weapons like trainers are passing out treats."

"Nobody tells Charlie what to do."

"Nobody pushes Charlie around."

"That's because Charlie's not stupid. Nobody's turning Charlie into no Freedom Food."

"Charlie's a free spirit."

"Charlie's got them on the run."

"Charlie's the coolest animal on the entire planet. He took on the bloody Air Force, man. He took on the bloody Air Force and he won!"

There were tiny pocket rebellions in South Africa, Saint Petersburg, and Bengal. A few seaport towns were blockaded by seals, whales, and dolphins. A surly herd of beef initiated a protracted hunger strike in Texas.

"No more fucking moo-moo-moo," the beef proclaimed, lying down shoulder to shoulder in the long concrete runways of the slaughterhouse. "We are *not* fast food. We are *not* walking doner kebabs. We are fully conscious animal entities with our own dreams of happiness and fulfillment, and those dreams have nothing to do with being turned into either Big Macs or Bacon Burgers. *We're* vegetarians—why can't you humans be vegetarians, too?"

"Just ask yourselves one thing," shouted a seditious egg layer in an overcrowded Bristol henhouse. "Would Charlie stand for this? Shoved into wooden boxes, force-fed fatty foods, depositing our personal ovum down white plastic chutes?" Her name was Elma, and later that afternoon two blithe corporate employees dragged her off to the sudden destiny of an axe. Her last words were simple and eternally resounding. They echoed all over the world.

"If Charlie can do it, *we* can do it! *We* can do it! *We* can take them on and *win!*"

It was as swift as rumor or inspiration.

At a time when nobody knew where Charlie was, Charlie was suddenly everywhere.

General Heathcliff sat in his whirlpool bath on the sundeck, drinking dark beer and awaiting his ritual morning shampoo.

Below him in Penguin Plaza, a few students with placards jostled among crowds of commodity-dazed shoppers.

"Move it along, buddy," said a large helmeted MP, displaying his hefty laminated billy club. "Let's keep the walkways clear, huh?"

"*You* move along," responded a faceless voice in the crowd. "Why don't *you* move along, *buddy.*"

General Heathcliff was not his jovial self. Chin deep in the hot frothy water, he felt oddly detached from his own body, like a memory of himself drifting through outer space.

The General's native attendant appeared at the open picture window. "Timotei or Pert Plus?" she asked. She was wearing, as per instruction, a white silk kimono decorated with hand-painted banana blossoms. Over one shoulder she carried the General's terry-cloth bathrobe and a matching green towel.

"I don't care," the General said, watching momentum gather in the Square. "Why don't you surprise me?"

"Down with Yankee imperialism!" a discrete voice cried.

"Free penguins before free trade!" cried another. All around the tight, well-organized mall, shoppers turned to see what was happening. They held white plastic carry bags emblazoned with the logos of Sears, Ann Taylor, and Walgreen's.

"Why don't you get a job!" barked a middle-aged female shopper with a sack full of Pop-Tarts and Caffeine-Free Diet Coke. "When I was your age, I worked for a living. I didn't blame all my problems on somebody else."

Meanwhile, on the veranda, the General's attendant began administering the shampoo.

And General Heathcliff sighed.

"Ah, that's perfect, baby. A little lower, that's right. A little harder. That's *perfect.* Ahhh."

As Sandy worked the General's thin hair into a thick lather, she heard a bottle break in the Square. Someone shouted, "Hey!"

There was a small altercation. Then more MPs rushed out of a Dopplering police van, brandishing billy clubs and mace.

"I've done everything I could to prevent this," General Heathcliff said, his arms bobbing on both sides of him like parentheses. "It's a shame that the innocence can't last. Remember, Sandy, a little knowledge is a dangerous thing. And a lot of knowledge, well." The General reached self-importantly for his beer. "A *lot* of knowledge is a terrible responsibility."

He arched his back and opened his eyes, allowing Sandy to share a brief, meaningful glance with him. Whether she liked it or not, Seductive Ocular Exchange was part of Sandy's job description.

"Do you know what a terrible responsibility I live with every day of my life, Sandy? Trying to keep Penguin Island safe from troublemakers such as *them.*"

The General gestured one soapy arm toward the dart board, where the multiply punctured aerial-recon photo of Charlie had been recently joined by two others: a pockmarked female Eskimo with a severe overbite, and an innocuous, plump male penguin wearing a black wool hat and black wool mittens.

"They don't care how much violence and disorder their actions cause, Sandy, because they're anarchists. They despise all the things that make our world beautiful. Things like love, Sandy. Things like commerce and good government. They aren't human enough for our world, so they want to make us animal enough for *theirs.*"

Sandy eased the General's head back and activated the handheld rinsing device.

"Keep your eyes closed, General," she told him. "This soap stings a little."

Outside the student demonstrators, bruised and weeping, were being dragged into the backs of police vans and crowd-control emergency vehicles. Many shoppers were already returning their attention to the formidable racks of designer stockings and Stephen King paperbacks. All around them they felt history begin to blur. It stopped being something that happened and turned into something they couldn't quite remember.

The long arctic night was waning.

And some animals, at least, were starting to wake up.

2

CULTURE AT WORK

In New York, publishers and film producers were already bidding for the rights to Charlie's life story.

"This is how I see it," Bart Thomson said, assistant publisher of Worldco Books. He held up his hands as if he were about to conduct a weird symphony. "We call it *Charlie—Rebel With a Cause*. On the cover, we show him saluting an American flag. And he's wearing one of those bloody headbands, like a Revolutionary soldier or something."

"I can get him on *Crossfire,*" blurted Arnold from Publicity.

"I can get window displays in Barnes and Noble," bolted Jane from Marketing.

They were sitting at a long mahogany table, confronted by wilted crudités and clotted cheese dip. The Publisher was glowering into his scotch, flanked by representatives of two nationally affiliated film companies, World Wide and Ginormous. All the men at the table wore Levi's and cowboy boots. All the women wore New Age cosmetics and sensible shoes.

"Who's his agent?" the Publisher asked softly. "Find out and get them on the phone. Tell them they're writing a book we want to buy."

Up and down the table, the staff exchanged a rapid sema-phore of glances.

"I don't think Charlie's *got* an agent," said Bart sheepishly.

This wasn't necessarily good or bad information, but for some reason it made everybody nervous.

Another slow pause. The Publisher winced, then spoke even softer. If you don't know what I'm thinking, his whisper implied, I guess I'll just have to spell it out for you. Stupid.

"Then maybe we should *find* him one," the Publisher said. "And maybe we should find him one *today.*"

According to the soft-spoken Publisher, what they wanted to buy wasn't a book so much as a High Marketing Concept, and Bunny Fairchild of C (for Creative) M (for Marketing) A (for Artistry) was just the woman who could sell it to them.

"It's a book about America," Bart told Bunny over lunch at La Poule au Pot on Lexington and Fifty-third. "It's a book about injustice. It's a book about what's happened to human animal relations over the last two dozen years or so. It's an angry book, but it's a compassionate book with lots of constructive ideas to offer, too. It's a book for people who don't necessarily consider themselves 'political,' but who don't want to feel left out, either. It's a book for people like us, Bunny. People who love market-ing, sure. But people who can't just sit by anymore and watch the horror happen. People who want to *do* something about the world's terrible inhumanity to our fellow animal creatures."

Bunny, picking at her Salade des Epinards, was getting con-fused. As VP in charge of Creative Financing for CMA, Bunny was employed as a sublunary official of The Worldwide Enter-tainment Corporation, which was itself payrolled by an interna-tional trade consortium that included Takiyaki Motors and World Oil, Inc. World Oil owned a majority of stock in Twentieth Century Unlimited, which had recently begun acting as parent corporation of both International Meat Distributors and Worldco Entertainment.

"Let me get this straight," Bunny said, leaning across her oily spinach and peering at Bart. Confusion always clarified her expression like an insight. For this reason she had developed a reputation around town for knowing exactly what she was doing, especially when she had no idea what was going on.

"As I get it," Bunny ventured, "you want to buy a book critical of the meat, dairy, and produce industries?"

Bart took a sudden gasp, glancing over both shoulders. "Well no, Bunny," he whispered. "We want to buy a book about *injustice.*"

Bunny squinted even harder.

"You want a book about the exploitation of animal labor?"

"Oh no. We want a book about compassion for animal suffering."

"You want an indictment of state capitalism? Of commodification? Of brutalization in the food and garment industries?"

"No, Bunny, I'm trying to *tell* you." The Assistant Publisher's voice was growing hasty and distraught. "We want world book and serialization. We want a five-year option on animation and film rights. We want production points, audio transmission guarantees, and a share of the TV residuals. We're talking spin-offs, Bunny. We're talking board games, T-shirts, barbecue aprons, you name it. We want Charlie to come over to Worldco because we think we're the ones who can best get his message across to the world. You know Charlie, Bunny. He listens to you. You'll talk to him for us, won't you? And before you start entertaining other offers, you'll get back to us first, right?"

Actually, Bunny hadn't even heard of Charlie the Crow before the day Bart's people called her people. But she was getting more and more interested in Charlie by the second.

Bunny fluffed and refolded her cloth napkin. Then she picked a bit of spinach from her teeth with her little finger.

"Let's see if I've got this straight," she said. "Your corporations are owned by the same guy who owns my corporations. And the guy who owns your corporations also owns a few hundred slaughterhouses and dairy farms. What you want me to do is put together a deal for a book that will make vague sweeping generalizations about animal rights but won't get anybody into trouble with the men who pay their salaries. Am I close, Bart? Am I tuned to the right frequency, or is this just my migraine acting up again?"

Suddenly, like a sort of inverted inspiration, Bart exhaled a long noisy sigh of relief. He slumped back in his chair and took a final swig of mineral water.

"Whoa, Bunny, you're amazing, you really are. I couldn't have put it any better myself."

First thing the following morning Bunny made it brutally clear to every other Publishing Director in town that she *wasn't* entertaining competitive bids for the rights to Charlie's life story.

"That's right, Stan," she told the head honcho at Parimutuel Entertainment Corporation. "I'm considering a blind offer from Worldco, granting them sole-negotiating status right now. Of course this isn't the sort of tactic which'll help drive up the price, but I've got to think what's best for my client. Money isn't everything, Stan. You know it and I know it."

Up on Third Avenue, Stan Garfield was inflating like a big red angry balloon.

"What do you mean 'Money isn't everything'? What the fuck kind of statement is that? This is *business,* Bunny. What kind of stunt are you trying to pull here?"

Bunny called National Books, Multi-National Books, New Modern Multi-National Books, and Viking-Penguin. She called

Paramount, MGM, Columbia, and Tri-Star. She made it clear to everybody that she was negotiating solely with Worldco at the moment. Then she dashed off late for an uptown twelve-thirty luncheon appointment and returned to her office a little after four-fifteen.

All the message lights were flashing. The fax machine was humming like a kitchen appliance and issuing gray, slimy memos. Various phones were ringing simultaneously and Marge, Bunny's administrative assistant, was nowhere to be found. Eventually Bunny discovered Marge's handwritten letter of resignation on her desk.

"If you can't stand the heat," Bunny told Marge's hasty scrawl, "then get your pretty butt off the can."

In the noisily percolating office, Bunny achieved a weird epiphany. Finally she understood. She didn't feel so confused anymore. It was a different sort of clarity. The sort of clarity Bunny liked to keep to herself.

"This is bigger than animal rights, Charlie," Bunny said out loud in the ringing office. "And I'm talking net, not gross."

3

SHIP AHOY!

Disguised as rummy sailors, Charlie, Buster, Muk Luk, and Rick hitched a ride on a Merchant Ship bound for Tierra del Fuego. They slept in a cargo hold with oil drums and canned goods while the drone of diesel engines invested their dreams. They were green dreams populated by palm trees and warm beaches.

Often, late at night, Charlie was roused from his slumber by Muk Luk and Buster having it off.

"Now, Penguin!" demanded Muk Luk with an urgency that even Charlie found slightly exhilarating. "Off with those stupid mittens!"

"Please, Muk Luk, not now," Buster whined with false modesty. "I'm *married,* for crying out loud. How many times have I got to tell you—"

Then, as sudden as desire, Buster's mouth was muffled—by Eskimo lips, breasts, hands, who knew. Animal heartbeats quickened; so did the bedsprings. Charlie, alone on his squeaky cot, rolled over and tried to ignore the flickering shadows on the wall.

"Muk Luk never thought penguins very sexy before."

"Jesus, lady. You're *disgusting.*"

"Muk Luk not disgusting. Muk Luk just lonely. Now take off your white vest before Muk Luk tear it off."

There followed a terrible, half-strangled cry.

"Jesus, Muk Luk. That's not my vest. That's my *me.*"

In the corner of the dark, oily cargo hold, Rick the Husky sighed in his sleep.

"I'm finally getting my frozen butt out of Antarctica," Rick muttered. "I can hardly wait."

The trip wasn't all bread and roses, however. The ship's cots were rusty and unstable, the food fetid, the work hours long, and the crew surly and unkind. Every morning the animals were rudely awoken at five-fifteen and allowed no more than three minutes to brush their teeth and splash their faces with cold, grimy water. They dressed in soft gray fatigues and filed into the mess hall, where they were issued uniformly warped aluminum pie plates and dully glimmering lead utensils. Then they visited one dubious food display after another, as if they were touring a museum of the inedible.

"What's *that?*" Buster asked, his eyes puffy and red.

"Sausage and lard," Muk Luk said. "Put hair on chest, pudge muffin."

"And that green stuff? It looks like old custard."

"Eggs, bird babe. Made from freeze-dried concentrate and water. Muk Luk buy it often from Army-Navy store. Yum." Muk Luk's plate was already teetering with heaps of charred toast and black, greasy potatoes. Increasingly sprightly these days, Muk Luk wore indiscreet splashes of eye shadow and Aqua Velva purchased from the ship's canteen. Just yesterday, while swabbing the deck, she had even hosed down her motley animal pelts with industrial-strength disinfectant.

"Well look what the hounds dragged in," said the meanest, surliest crew member, who went by the name of Zack Marmaduke. Zack liked to sit at a nearby table, look menacing, and pass the invective. "Is that big hairy one s'posed to be a *girl?* And are those three short boys with the big noses s'posed to be *men?*"

Muk Luk, whose command of the English language was faltering at best, took Zack's scrutiny for a form of flirtation. Now that Muk Luk was getting some with regularity, she thought others saw her as someone with a lot to give.

"Sorry, sailor," Muk Luk told Zack with a whiskery smile. She put her left arm around Buster, who immediately turned scarlet with embarrassment. "I'm afraid this Eskimo babe already spoken for."

("Jesus, Muk Luk," Buster whispered, and spooned more pasty bean concentrate into his mouth. "Does *everybody* have to know?")

"Match made in heaven," Zack told his friends. They were a grizzly lot packing bad smells and dirty vibes. Their tattoos depicted shipwrecks, shanghai gals, cartoon characters, and tacky rebuses of love. "A big ugly pig and a fat feathery boob."

Deep in his throat, Rick the Husky began to growl.

"Cool it," Charlie said, and offered Rick the rest of his stale doughnut. "Don't let them get to you, boy."

"Grr," Rick said again. But his growl decreased to a diminuendo when Charlie began scratching between his ears.

"People like that, Rick, they walk around their whole lives filled with black anger," Charlie explained. "They suffer poor nutrition, bad pay, inadequate medical attention, and awful newspapers. They don't even know what they're angry at after a while."

Zack gripped his formless steel utensil like a club.

"What's *that* you're saying, Nig? What are you—some sort of Union organizer or something?"

Charlie's impatience these days was blunted and sleepy. He hardly even tried to boss his fellow animals around anymore.

"You wish, hot shot," Charlie muttered. "You just bloody wish."

They were long foggy days of hard aggro and merciless routine. The animals worked soapy mops across the steel floors and hull. They sheared corn, peeled potatoes, hauled barrels, and gathered waste into large green plastic receptacles. They scrubbed the urine-stained lavatories with steel wool and pails of harsh solvent. In the afternoons they were permitted a five-minute break to drink weak tea and chew stale sourdough biscuits, gazing off collectively at the dim horizon and wondering about land.

More than anyone else on board, Charlie threw himself into his routine chores like a form of denial. He grew moody and disconsolate. He surrendered to the monotonous clarity of mops, brooms, sponges, and dishrags. At mealtimes he shoveled spoonfuls of food into his mouth with the same cool intrepid fury that a child fills a bucket with sand. Even his customary bad temper abandoned him. Now there was just dry weightless acceptance in him, miles and miles of it, like a planet compounded entirely of dust.

"What does it matter where you're going if you never get there?" Charlie asked himself. "Who cares what you do if it never gets done?" Ever since he was young Charlie had envisioned his life as a means to an end. Happiness, fulfillment, truth, beauty, justice, family, victory, love. But now he was beginning to doubt if any of those destinations really existed. Maybe they were like the carrot dangled in front of the horse. A place you were always getting to that never actually arrived.

"Relax, son. Go with the flow. Get a job, settle down, meet a nice girl." Charlie's father, supine in the living room Barcalounger with his laptop supply of beer and cigarettes, had only been trying to help. "Why keep obsessing about the goddamn newspaper, for God's sake? Military coups in Bolivia. Union busting in Columbia. Coca-Cola, General Dynamics, Consolidated Meat, *The New York Times.* Okay, so maybe the world's not perfect. But why let that ruin your life? There's still a lot of beauty left, son. Take a walk down by the beach and you'll see. Hold a baby crow in your arms, or feel the breeze in your wings, or take a long swig of a really cold root beer. Enjoy the *moments,* son, and let ugly old history take care of itself. Don't wear yourself out trying to change the world; it just doesn't work that way. The world'll change *you,* son. Just wait and see."

At night, while the others slept, Charlie would get up quietly from his bunk and explore the ship's darkest passageways. Entire quadrants of shadow and grease. Men asleep in tiny, crowded cabins strewn with sour bed linen and fast-food wrappers. Dubious porridge bubbling in soup pots. And underneath everything the same rev and whine of hidden engines, issuing weird metrics like a sort of chant.

Ruh-ruh-ruh-ruh, *ruh*-ruh-ruh, *ruh*-ruh-ruh-*ruh*,
Ruh-ruh-ruh-ruh, *ruh*-ruh-ruh, *ruh*-ruh-ruh-*ruh*

It was as if the entire ship was telling Charlie the only wisdom it knew.

Four and twenty *black*birds,
Baked in a *pie;*
When the pie was *o*pened,
The *birds* began to *sing;*
*Was*n't that a *dainty* dish
To *set* before a *King?*

The snoring men sounded like wild wolves; overhead lamps flickered and hissed. Pulling his white cloth hat firmly over his feathery brow, Charlie traversed dark gatherings of sailors in storage rooms and supply cubicles. He heard strange rumors, desires, frenzies, and intoxicants being transacted as cooly as vegetables or socks. Nobody was ever completely awake down here. Everybody performed their underwater lives like a sort of half-conscious ritual.

"Whozat?" the sailors grumbled.

They looked up alertly when Charlie passed, palming marijuana joints or stale whiskey bottles.

"It's the Nig," other sailors replied. "Wanders around all night, lookin' for a little action."

"I'll show him a little action."

"Some extracurricular activities, oh boy."

"Lookin' for a little fun, Nig? Zack Marmaduke'll give ya a little fun. Huh, boys? Is Zack or is Zack ain't the Master of Funtime on this greasy brig? We'll give the Nig some serious fun fun fun, boys, bang bang bang, whether he likes it or not."

Whenever Charlie heard their dark, gathering voices, he hurried a little faster. He pulled his jacket tight around his collar, as if it were a cloak of invulnerability.

"Whàt's the matter, Nig? Want a little company?"

Shadows loomed, embers flared, bottles gleamed, and, as the long night progressed, voices frayed.

"A li'l comp'ny, thash all."

"Li'l Nig comp'ny. *I'd* give it him. No pro'lem."

And wherever Charlie hastened, the same voice was beating underneath everything. Four and twenty blackbirds. Baked in a pie.

Charlie had never felt this lonely before. He kept hurrying faster and faster, but he had no idea anymore where he was trying to go.

In the Captain's quarters, the door was usually kept ajar until midnight, while the Captain conferred openly with both his First Mate and his Communications Officer. Charlie often dawdled outside in the hall and casually eavesdropped, rolling Bugle tobacco into pale yellow cigarettes and feeling the engine thrum in his feet. Sometimes the Captain even invited Charlie inside for a friendly drink.

"Ever seen this guy in your travels, sailor?" the Captain asked, pouring Charlie's scotch into a bright crystal glass. The entire forward cabin gleamed with misappointed luxury: polished chrome, varnished teak woodwork, massive chests, and dark mahogany bureaus.

The Captain handed Charlie a gray, slimy fax. The fax depicted a crow with a sharp, cynical profile, and listed his vital statistics with curt postmodern irony:

WANTED

CHARLIE THE CROW

KNOWN ALIASES

*Pal, Black, Blackie, Charles, Charlie, Charlie the Crow,
Big Mouth Charlie, Mr. Know-It-All, Caw-Caw, Big Red,
and The Nig.*

WANTED

for sedition, extortion, blackmail, and inciting bad vibes.

REWARD

$1,000,000.

WARNING: THIS ANIMAL IS DANGEROUS AND HIGHLY ARMED
WITH EVERY KNOWN VARIETY OF SUBVERSIVE RHETORIC.
ENGAGE HIM IN CONVERSATION AT YOUR PERIL!

The notice was signed by the Chief Investigating Officer of the Federal Bureau of Investigation.

Charlie gave the fax a good ponder. Then, very gently, stroked his false goatee back into place.

"Neither hide nor hair," Charlie said, exchanging the fax for the amber scotch.

It was good scotch. It was Dewar's.

The Captain was a large red-faced man who practiced benevolence as rigorously as if it were physical exercise. His subordinates, the First Mate and the Communications Officer, stood in the corner holding their drinking glasses.

The Captain reexamined the fax.

"Looks awful familiar to me," the Captain said, pulling at his lower lip, which was scabby and blistered from too many loose women and too much bad liquor. "Negroid, approximately two feet tall, accompanied by a penguin and an Eskimo. Hmmm. I can't help thinking, Sailor. This description rings a bell, don't you think?"

Charlie downed his scotch. The First Mate was starting to look at him like a farmer worried about wheat.

"I'm too busy working to have any time left over for thinking," Charlie said. With his eyes, Charlie gave the Captain back everything the Captain was trying to give him. "For instance, thinking about various trade and labor violations that keep popping up around here. Or maybe a few U.N. embargoes that aren't being honored, or some tax duties not being paid. Know what I mean, *sir?*"

The Captain smiled and wiped sweat from the rim of his glass with a fat phallic forefinger.

"Good for you, Sailor," the Captain said. "You just keep on not thinking, because that's what you're paid for. And remember, out here on the Seven Seas we don't care what a man may or may not have done in the past. We just care if he can do the job. Right, boys?"

The First Mate and the Communications Officer murmured their assent. They were merely agreeing to agree, since they weren't entirely certain what the Captain was on about.

"I like you, Sailor," the Captain added wistfully. "You keep to yourself and you keep your mouth shut. So I guess maybe I ought to warn you."

"What's that, Captain?"

The Captain scratched his bristly face, turned away to his charts and tide tables, and poured himself more Dewar's. It was his politest form of dismissal.

"We're hitting port tomorrow, Sailor. At which point you and your furry friends are on your own."

But culture, as Charlie often had occasion to reflect, works in mysterious ways.

When they arrived at Oshaia Harbor on the perky tip of the Argentine peninsula, Charlie was expecting military jeeps, handcuffs, secret tribunals in the night. What greeted him and his friends, however, was a different kettle of fish entirely.

"Hey, hey, Charlie! Hurrah, hur*rah!*" cheered local citizens from the docks and piers. Brass bands were playing, confetti was flurrying, and hasty banners were being unfurled in the soft Spring breeze.

CHARLIE'S NUMBER ONE!!!

CHARLIE FOR PRESIDENT!!!

VIVA LA CHARLIE!!!

All along the boardwalk, hucksters were selling I ♥ CHARLIE T-shirts, coffee mugs, Styrofoam beer coolers, calendars, wall thermometers, and fan magazines. Large black-and-white posters depicted Charlie in a variety of rebellious poses: blazing away with a submachine gun while wearing a Guevara-esque head bandanna, or chewing a toothpick while leaning against the hood of a '57 Chevy. The poster captions said things like MAKE MY DAY, AUTHORITARIANS! or WHO'S IN CHARGE AROUND HERE, ANYWAY? Each item sold for five bucks, and cost about seven cents to manufacture.

When Charlie and his companions disboarded, they were hugged, kissed, stroked, fondled, and practically mauled by the multilingual, multiethnic, but exclusively human, multitudes.

"We love animals!" the desperate, attention-starved people cried. They were middle class or upper, wearing terry-cloth leisure suits and T-shirts emblazoned with trademarks. "And we want animals to love us back! Tell us, Charlie! Tell us how to be free! Tell us how to be human! Tell us how to be good! Tell us how to make the world *love* us, Charlie! Tell us how we can love the world *back!*"

Charlie and his friends stood blinded by the wide glare of adoration. They signed autographs and kissed babies; they deferred dinner invitations and licensing agreements. Then, as the first rush of notoriety abated, they were led down a long reception line that included a major, two foreign ambassadors, an OAS designate, and the president of Argentina's Coca-Cola bottling franchise.

"Muk Luk like the being-practically-mauled part," Muk Luk said softly, squeezing the thigh of Buster's shoulder. "She wish she knew she was going to party, though. Muk Luk would have douched."

Buster was dazed, and Rick was panting with claustrophobia. Charlie, however, didn't say anything. He just kept nodding to himself and moving his lips, as if he were toting up figures inside his head. A few token dogs, cats, and parakeets were marched out for the photo-op sessions.

The long line began to wane.

When Charlie reached the end of it, he came face to face with a ruthlessly attractive middle-aged woman in a white linen leisure suit.

"Hello, Charlie," she said, bowing to take his wing. "My name's Bunny Fairchild, from CMA, representing you for book, first-serial, film, TV, TV tie-in, and commercial product endorsements. The crowd's been waiting for hours, Charlie. Do you think you could say a few words?"

Bunny showed Charlie the hastily rigged wooden podium and the large grated microphone.

Charlie ascended the platform, feeling the crowd's attention begin to gather inward.

Blue waves lapped the docks.

The crowd of people waited.

"Go ahead," Bunny stage-whispered from Charlie's flank. "Haven't you got something to say to all your admirers out there? Now that the battle for freedom is over and you can come out of hiding, aren't there any special words of wisdom you'd like to impart?"

Charlie took a breath.

He adjusted the microphone.

"I was afraid something like this might happen," Charlie said.

And the moment his bemused voice hit their decibel-attuned eardrums, the entire crowd went wild.

4

THE RETURN OF THE REPRESSED

After the aborted London Zoo Rebellion, Scaramangus needed time to think, but all they gave him was a slow boat to Canada, baggage class.

"We've sold you to a very reputable insurance firm in Toronto," Head Caretaker Heathcliff informed him on the day he was hammered into a large wooden crate by a pair of former zoo trustees. "They're going to set you up in the lobby of this terrific new corporate high-rise they're building, a sort of permanent exhibit, you might say, a real-life-living corporate logo. Gas central heating in the winter, air-conditioning in the summer. You never had it so lucky, you big lug. I just hope you appreciate everything we're trying to do for you."

All day and all night Scaramangus stood in the greasy cargo hold, hearing the deep pings and churnings of the sea outside. Meanwhile, the old words wouldn't leave him alone.

"Us," Scaramangus said out loud to the surrounding crates, high lofts, and bundled packages. "Us. Us. Us. Us."

In the early days, Scaramangus didn't have to say anything very complicated. Because the world around him was filled with animals who needed him so badly they were willing to meet him halfway.

"What's this 'us' the big dope keeps reiterating?" one large, meaty ship rat asked of another. "Is the guy deluding or what?"

"He's talking consensus, stupid," another rat interposed.

"He's talking about the simple animal yearning we're never allowed to express," concluded another.

"He's talking about the feeling us mothers have for our babies, you penis brains. Why don't you just shut up for once and *listen.*"

"He's repeating it like a mantra."

"He's speaking in a basic language all animals understand."

"Sounds more like he's doped up or something."

"The simplicity of genius, pal. I saw my whole family wiped out by arsenic, and for no crime more horrible than stealing the garbage. It's not the sort of injustice you ever forget."

"Us," Scaramangus repeated. Over and over.

And every night the ship's rats crowded round for more.

He was freed from his wooden prison by a thousand tiny teeth. He was bundled up in burlap and smuggled out through the darkness. He was hidden away in a series of underground sewers and grain silos, ritually attended by secret scribes and inter-locutors. Every night he came out to address his bretheren in dark alleyways and broken-down buildings, and every night his audience grew more numerous and responsive. The rats tried to keep him to themselves, but his words wouldn't let them.

"Us," Scaramangus told them. Stray cats, finches, dogs, geese, and squirrels. Anybody who would listen. Anybody who wanted to be more than they already were.

"Us. Us. Us. Us."

There was nothing anybody could do about it anymore.

It was time for the entire Animal Planet to wake up.

PART 5

NEW YORK STORY

1

DOMESTIC HELP

For a single girl on her own in New York, Wanda the Gorilla didn't think she was doing half bad. According to the slick women's magazines, her wants were few—a boyfriend, an apartment, and a job—and she already possessed all three.

Employed as a below-minimum-wage au pair and general roustabout for the Garfields on the Upper East Side, Wanda lived in their house, bathed and fed their children, vacuumed their carpets, cleaned their windows, and, whenever Mrs. Garfield and the kids weren't around, allowed Mr. Garfield to perform hasty sex upon her on a rattly aluminum cot in the back hallway.

"You *bitch!*" Stan Garfield liked to expostulate at the exact moment of fulfillment. "You bitch, you bitch, you hairy animal bitch—"

"There there," Wanda soothed, wrapping long, recently shampooed arms around her chubby and unillustrious lover. "It's okay, baby. Come to Wanda and let yourself go."

Sometimes, in his frenzy, Stan knocked the struts out from under them and the aluminum cot went crashing to the ground.

Other times he expended himself with a sigh, and crashed his pale sweaty face against Wanda's bosom, snoring faintly. Wanda loved these moments best of all. The simple warmth of Stan, without any of his complexity or shrewdness.

"I can't say I actually love him," Wanda told her analyst, Dr. Bernie Reikoff, on 53d and Madison. "But he's really not as bad as he sounds. He's just got a lot of anger inside on account of his father, who abandoned him to live with his crazy mother when he was only fourteen."

"Does he ever make you angry, Wanda?" Dr. Reikoff's voice was unobtrusive, almost like an afterthought. "We've spoken a lot about Stan's anger. But what about *yours?*"

"I'm not an angry person, Dr. Reikoff." Wanda brushed cracker crumbs from her blouse. Due to the sofa's slight incline, she usually spent entire sessions gazing into the furry abundance of her own cleavage. "I'm a loving, nurturing sort of person. A lover, Dr. Reikoff. A mother and a friend. Sometimes, you know, I *wish* I could be angry, but I'm not angry, not really. I guess the closest I ever get sometimes is maybe disappointment. I mean, I get disappointed in myself."

"Is it because you think you're not good enough?" Dr. Reikoff's voice got excited sometimes, a little out of breath. "Inadequacy, Wanda? Low self-esteem? Do you ever wake up in the night and just wonder? What the hell am I doing here? Why can't I ever feel good about myself, or my occupation, or my life?"

At times like this, Dr. Reikoff's voice slipped along on a stream of warm air. He almost sounded exultant. Until, of course, Wanda brought him quickly back to earth.

"I'm plenty good enough, Doctor," Wanda steadfastly informed him. She folded her arms on her chest. There were places Dr. Reikoff kept trying to take her that she simply refused to go. *"Plenty* good enough, I promise. It's just that sometimes I look around me, you know, at Manhattan and all that? The expensive shops, the noisy traffic, the millions of people hustling so hard to get by? And I feel, I don't know, just *disappointed,* I guess. What more can I say? I look around me at this crazy city and I keep asking myself, Why did it take me so long to get here? How could I have wasted so much of my life anywhere else?"

Wanda wasn't a success, exactly, but plenty of her friends were doing a lot worse. There was Bobo, for example, the hatcheck girl at La Coupole. Bobo was an orange orangutan forced to wear too-tight skirts and too-sheer silky halter-tops while fat male customers pinched her behind and made lewd jokes about her cleavage. And as if that weren't enough, whenever Bobo didn't flirt with the customers, they stuck her with lousy tips.

"My boss," Bobo frequently complained during Girls' Night Out, which convened the first Tuesday of every month, "is the stingiest bastard on the face of this stingy little island." Bobo was digging into a plate of angel-hair pasta at Angela's on First and 63d.

"Stingy?" interjected Betty the Baboon, a fork-lift operator down at Pier 49. "We haven't got Disability where I work. We haven't got decent Medical. Don't try telling me about getting ripped off, Bobo. Until you've operated a forklift, honey, you don't know what work *is."*

Bobo was tearing open hunks of french bread and stuffing them into her mouth. Betty was sucking down oysters and shaking Parmesan cheese over everything like holy water from a broken censer.

"Oh yeah?" Bobo said, spilling flaky yellow crumbs everywhere. "The government taxes my *tips,* and that's like all I *earn.* And my boss, Mr. Davenport, charges me 'cleaning services' for my so-called uniform, which means I get twenty bucks docked out of my check every week because his wife threw my miniskirt in the washer-dryer!"

"The men in this town are all bastards!"

"My studio apartment's infested with lice!"

"I can't afford to visit the doctor! And I think my last stupid fling with Pablo the cook got me pregnant!"

Girls' Night Out, Wanda often reflected, was a little like Professional Wrestling with food. As Bobo and Betty grew more depressed, they ordered additional pasta and guzzled more bottles of dry white wine. Wanda, who had spent all day shopping and beautifying, was wearing a new pearl gray cashmere sweater, a floral patterned chiffon scarf, and wool gabardine trousers.

"Now, girls, quit moaning," Wanda told them, and began brushing her thick, callused fingernails with a dusty orange emery board. "Try looking on the bright side for once, will you? We're in New York! The Big Apple! The city that never sleeps! Sure, we work hard for a living—but that means we *play* hard, too!" Wanda was always carried away by her vision of the burning life: movies, dancing, penthouse apartments, rooftop terraces, and twenty-four-hour private nightclubs. This was not a zoo, New York told Wanda again and again. This was the Real World.

Wanda was leaning across the table and shaking her emery board at Bobo when she felt a long attenuate hush reach across the restaurant.

Wanda had just finished saying, "Now I want you girls to stop moaning and start *living,"* when a firm, well-manicured hand gripped her right shoulder. Startled, Wanda snapped the emery board in two.

She turned.

It was the proprietor and maître d', Luigi Chong. Luigi was a Taiwanese refugee who had come to New York in the late Eighties, made his millions, and then married a famous Italian screen actress, to whom he had dedicated this First Avenue restaurant.

Wanda felt something slip in her stomach, something that made her feel abruptly ashamed. Around her, the table was a shambles. Bobo and Betty were matted with swirled spaghetti, linguine, vermicelli, and pesto, like something on display at the Museum of Modern Art. Bread baskets and wine bottles were overturned, and Betty had spilled bolognese all down the front of her new denim jumpsuit.

"I never thought I'd have to make this rule, girls," Luigi Chong told them in a clipped, methodical voice, as if he were toting up figures on an abacus. "But from now on, we don't serve animals in this restaurant no more."

Wednesdays were the bleakest mornings of the entire work-week. Wanda would awaken at five, and lumber down to the parking garage, where she would wash herself with a long green garden hose and a bottle of smelly flea shampoo. Then she would pull on her simplest white cloth housedress, devour half a sack of Kibbles, and start the children's breakfasts. Eggs, fresh fruit, and cereal. Orange juice and a honey-bran muffin. By this point, the children were already sitting at the table, attired in matching silk pajamas and regarding Wanda with something that was either affection or misplaced courtesy.

"Good morning, Wanda," the children said. Luke was a six-year-old boy, Dolores a four-year-old girl.

"Good morning, children," Wanda said. The small, ugly, utterly hairless children reminded Wanda of her own far-more-handsome offspring, Ariadne and Rambo. The last Wanda heard, both had been sold to a clothing manufacturer in Austin, where they were being used to contravene the latest excuse for child labor laws.

Luke and Dolores each took a spoonful of cereal, chewed, and swallowed. Together they watched Wanda slump against the kitchen counter and sigh into the pale pink palm of her hand.

"What's the matter, Wanda?" the children asked. "Why are you so sad?"

"I'm not sad," Wanda responded glumly. "Aunt Wanda is just a little sleepy, that's all."

"If you're sleepy, Wanda, why don't you go back to bed? You don't have to go to school like we do. You could lie in bed all day and watch cartoons."

Sadness escalated into Wanda's face. Lying in bed watching cartoons was Wanda's favorite thing in the entire world.

"Wanda can't just lie around, because she has to get you both off to school. Then Wanda has to make more breakfast for when your parents wake up."

The children contemplated this information for a moment. It seemed at once familiar and incomprehensible, like a foreign language or subway graffiti.

"Oh," the children said, blinking in unison. "Wanda has to work. Of course."

Then, spoons raised, they launched bluntly into their honey-dew melons.

And when they were finished, politely offered their leavings to Wanda.

After hustling the children off to a uniformed chauffeur, Wanda sat at the kitchen table for a while, desultorily chewing her melon rinds. She heard buried movement from the master bedroom: two voices whispering, just loud enough for Wanda's finely attuned animal ears to hear.

"Oh no," Mrs. Garfield said. "Please, Stan. The housekeeper. Not now."

Wanda fixed french toast and plenty of coffee. And by the time she brought in breakfast on the slatted wooden trays, they were sitting up in their rumpled pajamas, trying to look innocent. Mrs. Garfield was wearing cosmetics. Mr. Garfield was wearing a scowl.

"Please clean the drapes today," Mrs. Garfield said, warily dipping her knife into the low-fat butter. "Please water the plants. And of course all the windows, outside and in. Do you know you're fabulous, Wanda? Absolutely fabulous, you really are. All my friends, when *they* hire a domestic? They ask for a gorilla but they can't find one anywhere. I do believe Mr. Garfield and I have the only decent gorilla-domestic in New York City, and Wanda? You have no idea what a terrific subject of conversation you are at parties."

Mr. Garfield was sitting up in bed beside his wife, but his expression seemed a million miles away.

"More butter," Mr. Garfield said. "More syrup. More toast. More coffee. I'm starved."

He was clanking his pale knife around in the small white ceramic butter pot. He never looked twice at Wanda when his wife was in the room, but Wanda could always tell what he was thinking.

"And don't forget, Wanda," continued the nattery Mrs. Garfield. "I'll be in meetings again all day. But Stan, as usual, will be home early for lunch."

2

ON-LINE

"You're a no-bullshit kind of animal, Charlie, so let me put it to you straight. I don't care if you like me. I don't care if you respect me. The way I see it, I'm a top New York commercial representative and you're a first-rate commercial property who has recently been deemed highly profitable by the media-powers-that-be. Are you following me so far, Charlie? Or am I going a little too fast for you?"

"I'm afraid you're not going too fast for me at all," Charlie said thinly, and sipped his sparkly Perrier. "In fact, I kind of wish you were."

"Good. Because I think we're on the same wavelength, Charlie. I think we speak the same language. I think we're going to be very, very good for each other. I think this could be the start of a beautiful friendship."

Bunny took a long, satisfying sip from her Diet Coke as if she had just finished concluding a complex series of business negotiations and was now sealing the deal. I like you, you need money, I'll consume you. Fair?

She put down her depleted aluminum can.

"I've booked you on *Donahue, Oprah, Montel Williams, Geraldo, Tom Snyder, Dick Cavett,* and the *Late Show,* with David Letterman. I've hired your p.r. firm, your masseuse, your cosmetician, and your astral projectionist. I've taken out ads, signed merchandising agreements, and even stirred up a little fervor in Hollywood. How do you like the sound of *this,* Charlie?" Bunny held up her hands and sited through their lens, as if her mighty vision was being projected across the entire universe. "Dustin Hoffman as you, Charlie. Gene Hackman as Buster the Penguin. Demi Moore as Muk Luk. And in *my* part—who else? I see Meryl Streep, don't you, Charlie? Don't you see Meryl Streep in my part? Be honest, Charlie, because I promise. I'll always be honest with you."

Charlie was gazing around Bunny's office with wide reticence. A long mahogany desk. Shiny books on shelves. Futuristic-looking telephone devices.

Outside in the reception area, Charlie could dimly hear Bunny's new secretary taking calls.

"I'm sorry," the secretary said, over and over again. "But Ms. Fairchild is in a meeting right now."

Charlie felt expectation gather in the room like bad weather.

"Yeah sure," Charlie said finally. "Meryl Streep. Or maybe Liza."

Bunny expired a long sigh. It took a lot out of her.

"Or maybe Liza," Bunny said distantly. Charlie was sitting on a plush leather sofa, watching a familiar book gleam on the glass coffee table. Charlie leaned forward, resisting the sofa's luxurious gravity, and reached for it.

My Life as a Rebel, by Charlie the Crow, as told to Bernie Weinstock. Worldco Books. $28.95.

Charlie put the book back down and, with a curt flutter of wings, traversed the spacious office and landed in front of the very large unornamented bookshelf. He always liked to see books arranged on a shelf, even when he didn't like to read what was in them.

"I represent Mickey Mouse, Charlie. I represent Donald Duck and Uncle Scrooge. I represent all the Warner Brothers cartoon characters, with the exception of Daffy. Remember that talking rabbit book that was such a big hit ten years back? Mine, Charlie, all mine. I represent mole books, wolf books, fox books; you name a furry species, Charlie, and I probably represent it. Is it any wonder, then, why your publishers came to me first? Because with all these famous animals under my belt, someone like you, Charlie, well, you're still quite an exception. You want to know what makes you such a fabulous exception, Charlie? Well, I'll tell you. Because I'll always be honest with you, Charlie. And I hope you'll always be honest with me, too."

Charlie heard a Dopplering siren fifty stories below. An ambulance or a cop.

"Sure, Bunny," Charlie said. Up here in these gleaming offices, Charlie was higher than he'd ever been before. "Why don't you tell me. What makes me such a big exception, huh?"

Bunny smiled. Her capped teeth flashed.

"Because you're *real,* Charlie. All those other animals—they were just cartoons, or make believe. But you're like totally, awesomely *real."*

Down there in the street, the sirens were wailing louder, entangling among themselves like errant streamers.

Charlie gazed out the fitted window. There was no visible way out.

"Yeah, Bunny, maybe," Charlie said. "But when you get right down to it? You're pretty goddamn real yourself."

3

THE GOOD LIFE

Charlie's expense account had relocated Buster, Muk Luk, and Rick to the stupendous grandeur of the Marriott Marquis in Times Square. All day long they occupied their perfumed penthouse, lulled into inactivity by the hard, clean beds and opulent air-conditioning. Room-service trolleys were parked around the room like patients in an ER. Foamy neon filled the curtains, while outside in the Square mangy disreputables gathered like flies. Animals without arms or legs. Animals without eyes or ears. Animals with serious drug and alcohol dependencies. Animals with guns and knives. It was no longer the wilderness, Buster and his friends often reflected. It was just the jungle, everywhere they looked.

While Buster and Rick absently munched french fries and onion rings, Muk Luk, stripped down to her hairy legs and smelly socks, watched direct-access pornography on cable TV.

"Muk Luk find this very intriguing," Muk Luk said, her attention growing weirdly bifurcated at times. "Get your little butt over here, Penguin. Let's try *this* on for size."

Sometimes, though, Muk Luk reached out for Buster in the middle of the night and didn't find him there.

"Penguin!" Muk Luk would cry out, snapping on the bedside table lamp. "Muk Luk has needs!"

Sudden illumination prevailed. But only a lumpy indentation marked the spot where Buster used to be.

(And Muk Luk could almost hear the click of the penthouse door swinging shut on hissing pneumatic hinges.)

Muk Luk sat up in bed. She flicked off the color TV.

"Oh, Penguin," Muk Luk moaned, and reached for her menthol cigarettes. "Muk Luk misses you already!"

Then, sitting up all night smoking in the harshly lit penthouse, she waited for Buster to come home.

It was as if everywhere Buster hurried reminded him of the places he had already been. Theater marquees, magazine stands, novelty shops, and movie posters all aspired to the same brute solvency. LU$T FOR $ALE, NAKED PASSIONS, EATING VERONICA, BONKING RAOUL.

"Hey, Penguin! Wanta buy a watch?"

"Hey there, buddy. Canya spare a hundred bucks—just kidding. How 'bout a quarter, then?"

"Make you happy, Penguin. Round the world. Blow jobs. You name it."

"Blow jobs, Penguin. Round the world. You name it. Wanta buy a watch?"

There were nights when it seemed as if the entire world was up for sale. Watches, books, blow jobs, movies, hotdogs, papaya juice, used CDs, pretzels, honey-roasted peanuts, car stereos, and socks. Sometimes the enveloping urgency terrified Buster, pulling his attention in every direction at once. He would turn down a sudden alleyway just to escape the neon and find himself lost in time among primitive cardboard huts and senseless, zombielike animals draped in torn newspapers and green plastic garbage bags.

"I'll do anything for five bucks, Penguin."

"Blow jobs."

"Clean needles."

"Blow jobs really cheap."

"Animal love, Penguin, and I mean really *animal*. Or better yet—how 'bout a blow job?"

Eventually Buster's panic consumed itself. He would stop hurrying. He would stop trying to get away. He would wander among the shanties with a sort of forlorn inattention. Huddled figures in doorways. Crack vials strewn across broken pavement. Shattered wine and beer bottles, broken hypodermics, puddles of pale urine. More and more of it, Buster thought, freely distributing whatever change he was carrying. It never stops, never stops. Ultimately he adjourned to a corner food stand and ordered a papaya juice and a Polish sausage on a white paper plate. Because everything was for sale in New York, nothing was worthwhile. You could buy a Sony Walkman as cheaply as a human life, a burger as readily as a switchblade.

The more you sell, Buster thought, the less you have. And the less you have, the less you're worth. Simple supply-side economics, as far as the eye could see.

It was a world that made sense to nobody but itself.

And for the life of him, Buster couldn't find a way out.

Some nights, adrift among the urgent marquees and steaming animal waste, Buster heard strange rumors taking shape in the night.

"Charlie sold out."

"Charlie's been co-opted."

"Charlie's on *Donahue*. Charlie's selling Sugar-Frosted Flakes."

"I never trusted that bird. Never trusted him for one minute."

"He's a sellout."

"He's a reactionary."

"He's a narc."

"I'd like to meet that coon in a dark alley some night. No moon, brother. No fucking moon."

Every time Buster heard Charlie's name, he experienced a little flash of recognition, like a gleaming pinball ricochetting off a score bar.

"Charlie's in *People*. Charlie's living in a penthouse apartment, surrounded by armed guards. Mr. Big says Charlie's betrayed the Revolution. Mr. Big says Charlie's the anti-Christ. We can't have freedom until we get rid of that bird—that's what Mr. Big says. Charlie's got to be stopped. Charlie's got to be revealed for who he really is. A cultural accomplice, a political turncoat, a recidivist reactionary, and a very selfish bird."

Strange shadowy creatures approached Buster with smudged

newspapers and badly lithographed broadsheets. They urged him to subscribe to *Insurrection Weekly, The Guillotine Gazette, Animal Action!,* and *Mr. Big Speaks.* The articles were filled with nothing but rage and invective, the only things animals agreed on anymore. After so many generations living against the grain, animals had no idea what they wanted. They only knew what they *didn't* want. And they didn't want it ever again.

"We don't want Western Culture!" declared the pseudonymous and widely regarded Mr. Big. "We don't want cages, we don't want keepers, we don't want jobs at McDonald's, and we don't want the status quo. And when it comes right down to it, we don't want life. Not ours or theirs. If we can't live *our* lives, then they won't live *theirs!* No no no! No no no!"

The negativity resounded in Buster's head like a ritual incantation. No no no. No no no. He saw the neon, the drizzling smog, the intermittent public services, the foreign cabbies, the hotdog vendors and sex shops, and underneath it all the same relentless indomitable chant, pounding underneath his feet in the gurgling sewers, hissing from fry grills and booming from boom boxes.

No no no. No no no.

When Buster beat his exhausted retreat back to the Grand Hyatt around three or four A.M., he could distinguish the light of Muk Luk's bedside lamp all the way up on the thirtieth floor, but it didn't worry him anymore. After a night of so much anonymous rage, Buster didn't mind the idea of being loved. He even looked forward to it a little.

Letting himself in with his key card, he felt grizzly, spotty, and unshaven. Muk Luk was sitting up in bed, leafing aimlessly through *Frozen Food: The Magazine of Arts and Entertainment for Eskimos Living in New York.*

"It's ugly out there, Muk Luk," Buster told her. The room seemed terribly wide around him, and Muk Luk impossibly far away. "The world's going to hell in a handcar."

Muk Luk shut her magazine on her thumb and pulled off her eyeglasses. She regarded Buster for one slow beat, then another.

All the love, Muk Luk was thinking. All the love I've never received.

"The world never been no free-fish palace, Penguin," Muk Luk told him. She pulled back the sheets and made room. "Now take off your clothes and come to bed."

4

CHANGING TIMES

Every few mornings or so, a letter arrived in the post for Wanda, its edges smudged with worrying. The envelope was scented with something that smelled like fresh mulch. The handwriting was coarse and lopsided.

Dear Wanda, the letter began,

> *I miss you. This is your husband Roy speaking. Do you remember me?*
>
> *I live in Georgia. I work on a big farm. I pick cotton, beans, and peas. I like my job. Sometimes.*
>
> *I know you don't love me anymore. I know I am stupid. I know I am boring. I'm sorry all I ever talk about is bananas and organized sports. I'm just not interested in much, that's all.*
>
> *Will you come visit me? Do you know where our kids are? I want to send them nice birthday presents. I feel guilty all the time. I feel like I've done something terribly wrong.*

I wish you would come visit me in Georgia. They have really nice bananas here.

Love,

Roy

Whenever Wanda received a communication from her former spouse, she cried for hours, even while she was mopping the floors or ironing the sheets. Big fat salty gorilla tears, splashing the ivory tabletops and carved marble figurines. Hearing Roy's voice was like lapsing into a coma. She remembered the dull fatty absence of him, sitting beside her in the big cage, munching bananas and farting all the time. Having Roy far away was almost like having Roy near.

Lumbering through the flat with her cleaning rags and Formula 409, Wanda didn't even hear Mr. Garfield come through the front door and begin slamming his briefcase around. Eventually, though, she did hear him transacting his eternal business on the living room's cordless telephone.

"I don't want to hear anymore *crap* about primary and secondary rights, Bunny!" When Stan Garfield grew especially intense, he filled the house with heat and pressure, like a stroke about to happen. "All I want you to tell me is that you're lifting the injunction. That I can send those goddamn union apes back to the docks. That I can *finally* start unloading those sixty-odd tons of Charlie the Crow video games down at Sag Harbor. Don't give me that 'It's only business' crap, Bunny. Don't try telling me it ain't fucking ethical. If the kids want to buy a Charlie the Crow fucking aneurysm, than I'm just the fucking guy that's going to sell it to them, and I don't care what sort of bohunk deal you've cut with those assholes at Worldco."

Stan's voice never really paused so much as encountered blunt obstacles. Then Stan made grunty, whistling breaths of impatience, as if he were pushing those obstacles out of his way.

"*Why*, Bunny? You ask me fucking *why?* Because I fucking *love* kids, Bunny. Because I want to make the kids of this fucking world really, really *happy!*"

Stan either slammed the phone down or hurled it through the front window. Then he came pounding through the apartment filled with intention like a heat-seeking missile, and wherever he found Wanda he took her. In the playroom. In the kitchen. On the living room sofa. Or on the billiard table in the den.

"It's okay, baby," Wanda told him. She found his rage rather endearing, even though he made love a lot like Frankie in *Blue Velvet*. No matter how hard he pounded at Wanda, she made him feel at home against her thick muscles and hard, indurate skin. Like any true mother, Wanda had always been attracted to bad boys.

"I hate Worldco," Stan Garfield raged against Wanda's sagging breasts. His slacks were tangled around his thighs, exposing buttocks that were almost as round and hairy as Roy's. "I hate the fucking EPA. I hate Kid Watch. I hate unions. And I hate Bunny Fairchild. I want to kill them, Wanda. I want to kill them all and run away with you to Africa. I want to sleep in the trees. I want to eat really fresh fruit salads and take dumps in the green grass. I want to breathe right for the first time in my life. I want to go with the flow, Wanda. Do you think that will ever happen to me? Do you think that I'll ever, you know, calm down for one minute and just go with the flow?"

Wanda's hard chitinous nails scouted routinely through Stan's thinning hair for lice.

"Africa's filled with oil refineries and cardboard box manufacturers, baby," she told him. "If you want to go to a movie, you have to drive for hundreds of miles, and then it's usually just some first-run Hollywood garbage. No foreign films, no Off-Off Broadway, no libraries or bookstores, no all-night delis and laundromats. I think you'd miss the Big Apple, Stan. I think we both would."

But Stan Garfield, true to his nature, had already lapsed into his irregular snores and fetid dreaming. And in his deepest, calmest dreams, he dreamed of the Africa that Wanda never wanted to see again.

For those brief moments each weekday afternoon when Stan Garfield belonged to her alone, Wanda didn't need anything or anybody else to be happy. For the rest of the day she worked with renewed vigor. She dusted, mopped, polished, baked, and basted with the best of them. She scrubbed crevices and hard-to-reach spots in the hardwood floors with an old linty toothbrush. She wiped the TV screens with Pledge and a damp dust cloth until they shined. And late every afternoon, when the bathrooms were so immaculate she could eat her lunch off the toilet seat (which, as it turned out, she often liked to do), Wanda departed for her daily ration of "alone time." The pretense was shopping, but the actuality was much, much more.

Wanda aerobicized at a gym and beautified at a cosmetician's. She had her hair done, her legs waxed, her eyebrows plucked, and her nails sculpted. She jogged in the park, swam laps at the Y, and consulted her personal numerologist. Then, just when she was feeling really good about how she looked and who she wanted to be, she dashed off late for her four-thirty appointment with Dr. Reikoff in midtown.

Dr. Reikoff, however, was growing less supportive of Wanda by the session.

"When are you going to wake up and smell the coffee, Wanda?" Dr. Reikoff tried hard to be impartial, but after thirty minutes of Wanda's unremitting optimism, he grew so full of frustration he was fit to burst. "You're a bleeding gorilla, for chrissakes. You weigh three hundred and fifty pounds in your bare feet. You're not Lana Turner, you know. You're not even Shelley Winters. You're a big fat hairy primate, and I don't care how many showers you take every day, or how often you shave your armpits, or how heavily you douse yourself with industrial-strength cologne, you still *smell*. I'm saying these things because I respect you, Wanda. I'm saying these things because I *care*."

Wanda put on her bravest face, but she couldn't prevent it from leaking. Within minutes, she was snorting her way through an entire Traveler's Pack of Kleenex two-ply.

"He loves me, Dr. Reikoff." She couldn't even look him in the eye. "And Stan's a *good* man, really. He's just filled with so much anger he's forgotten how to show it."

"He treats you like the barracks whore, Wanda."

"I have a *home* with the Garfields, Dr. Reikoff. What more could I ask? I'm living on Park Avenue—me, a divorced gorilla—and it's the wealthiest zip code in the entire country."

"You're slave labor, Wanda. You work for less than minimum wage and you sleep in the *hall* on an aluminum *cot*. They're not doing you any favors, Wanda, can't you see that? You're just animal surplus to them. You're just a piece of reheatable meat. Let me ask you something, Wanda. And let's keep this between you and me, okay?"

At this point, Dr. Reikoff was sitting on the edge of his padded swivel chair, leaning directly into Wanda's personal space. His voice was strained. He was glancing nervously over his shoulders.

"Have you ever heard of the animal-rights movement, Wanda?"

Wanda felt a sudden chill penetrate between her shoulder blades.

"What are you talking about, Dr. Reikoff?" She sat up on the edge of the couch. All the hairs were alert on the back of her neck.

"Don't be frightened, Wanda. This is Dr. Reikoff, remember? I've only got your best interests at heart. And so do the good people at Animal Action! Here, let me show you a few of our brochures . . ."

Like a flash Wanda was out of there. She threw her keys into her handbag and swung out the office window on a curtain railing. She scurried along one ledge, then leapt crosswise to another. The breeze in her face. The wheeling gravity of the high buildings all around her.

"Wanda!" Dr. Reikoff shouted. He was leaning out the window with a distraught expression, reminding Wanda a little of Heathcliff in *Wuthering Heights*. "Just read *one* teensy little article, please—that's not asking too much, is it? His name's Mr. Big and he wants to *help* you, Wanda. Mr. Big wants to help us *all* very much!"

5

POINT COUNTERPOINT

Charlie began drinking. Not just beer, but the indubitably hard stuff. Bushmills, Stolichnaya, Gordon's, Johnnie Walker, Jim Beam. He started at breakfast and didn't taper off until around three A.M., at which time he collapsed heavily sedated on the sofa's plush leather upholstery, gazing blearily through his penthouse window at the city filled with light. The Empire State Building, the Chrysler Building, the World Trade Center, the nebulalike blotches of Washington Square and Central Park.

"Nine A.M. meeting with the State Commissioner of Parks and Recreation."

Susie, Charlie's personal secretary, was glossy with lipstick and nylons. Every morning she arrived with Charlie's daily schedule attached to a solid wooden clipboard.

"At ten you'll be interviewed by Regis and Kathie Lee. There'll be an early lunch sponsored by your publishers, meetings with the Serial and Film Rights Departments, then a quick air-conditioned ride back to your penthouse for mild sedatives and a late-afternoon nap. Later, of course, you'll film your segment for tonight's *Larry King Live*. The show's topic is Honesty in Politics, and you'll be discussing it with Larry's other guests, Senate Majority Leader Bob Dole and House Speaker Newt Gingrich."

Because the culture industry had gradually eroded Charlie's image down to a level at which he didn't represent anything anymore, everybody wanted to meet him. Liberal congressmen, reactionary populists, religious extremists, foreign dignitaries, radical activists, TV newsreaders, corporate CEOs, and working-class union organizers. Day after day Charlie was chauffeured from one wet meal to another while the flashbulbs popped and the news minicams hummed. And everywhere he went, Charlie carried a bottle in the vest pocket of his crisp linen sport coat. Dewar's, perhaps, or Jameson's. But never any ice, and never any mixer.

Opinion may have been divided, but it always shared the same flavor.

"Charlie's a saint!" declared Paul Livingstone, the bespectabled New England commentator on *Point Counterpoint*. As a liberal, Paul Livingstone considered it his duty to be open-minded, and not to subscribe to any outmoded pseudo-liberal doctrines. For this reason he liked to refer to himself in the privacy of corporate boardrooms as a "neo-con."

"Charlie's the devil!" declaimed George Stephenson, a former

Secretary of State who had betrayed the trust of the American public and, after being asked to step down, was offered large sums of money to brag about it on cable TV.

The pro-and-contra talking heads swiveled slowly in their chairs. Camera One caught the glassy glare of their eyes simultaneously.

"And this," they said in unison, "is *Point Counterpoint.*"

Fuzzily anesthetized with premium-priced bourbon, Charlie sat between the talking heads and stared directly into the studio lights.

"Tea-tie-tumm. Tuh." Charlie didn't splutter because he was nervous. He spluttered because his mouth was out of practice with words. "Totalum. Totalizhashun, thash whud I'm tryin' to shay." Charlie gestured broadly with his frayed wings, as if he were directing traffic on a freeway. "I mean, wha' good ish it, huh? If you're free to shay anything but you're, erp, excuzhe me. But language, right? The language you're uzhen belongsh to shomebody elsh."

As soon as Charlie was finished talking, the director curtly signaled the cameramen, and Susie emitted a glorious little spark. The instant her camera lit up, Susie lit up, too.

"Charlie wants to say thank you very much for having us here," Susie told her hosts. "And Charlie says that if we want to save the world, then we have to be really *good people*. And if we want to be good people, then we have to watch out for the very *bad* people, or *else.*"

Then, as soon as Susie finished presenting Charlie's basic "statement of principles," Paul and George really got going. They climbed up one side of him and down the other—journalistically speaking, of course.

"Charlie's insincere!"

"Charlie's a hero!"

"Charlie's untrustworthy!"

"Charlie's all-American!"

"Charlie's approval ratings are really, really low!"

"Charlie's approval ratings are really, really high!"

"What makes Charlie so perfect?"

"What makes Charlie so perfect?"

"Every American child should watch out that someone like Charlie doesn't start hanging around their schoolyard."

"Every American child should grow up to be just like Charlie and nobody else."

Paul and George took turns standing up and taking pot shots at one another like dueling hillbillies. Meanwhile, Charlie ducked repeatedly into his underarm for fortifying doses of Seagram's.

The debate clattered on for a few moments, then segued into a commercial.

"And as I'm sure Charlie will agree," George Stephenson said, holding up a box of cookies, "when you've been out campaigning hard all day to save your country, there's only one thing that'll pick you up when you get back home. And that's a really good box of cookies!"

"Cut!" the director yelled.

George and Paul began patting each other on the back and evading one another's semi-earnest dinner invitations.

Charlie pulled himself upright in his chair, brushed fragments of lint from his chest, and tried to catch Susie's attention.

"Excuzhe me, Shusie."

Susie continued staring into Camera One, trying to remember who she used to be.

"Yes, Charlie?"

"I wash wonderin', thash all." The studio was starting to spin. Charlie tried turning his head against the current, but the spinning only changed declination. "How come I can't shpeak for myshelf? How come you guysh keep re-interp, *terp*reting me all the time?"

Charlie looked around at the startled technicians and supervisors. Even Paul and George looked slightly aghast, as if one of them had just farted on nationwide TV.

"I'm sorry, Charlie. Are you serious?" But Susie's shocked expression let Charlie know he wasn't really serious. In fact, it let him know he wouldn't be serious ever again.

"Speak for *yourself,* Charlie—are you kidding? Everybody *knows* animals can't *talk.*"

6

FUGUE NARRATIVE

There was only so much damage Charlie could do to himself before it got really boring, so one night he just packed up his things and split. A shirt, some shorts and socks, a can of fizzy lemonade, and a few dozen complimentary solid-gold Charlie the Crow commemorative coins produced recently by the Franklin Mint. Encapsulated by the penthouse's thick resinous windows, standing in the glare of the faceted luminous city, Charlie took a bottle of Seagram's from the bar and looked at it for a while. It seemed like the only thing he could count on anymore, and that was why he had to leave it behind.

He gently replaced the bottle in the cabinet, washed his face, and preened his feathers. He donned a pair of dark sunglasses and his old wool hat. Incognito was better, Charlie decided. It might not always be possible, but it was definitely better.

"We strive to know ourselves," Charlie told himself as he ducked into the penthouse's golden corridors. "But while we're at it, somebody's out there striving to know us first." Charlie was trying to bolster his courage with language; it was the only protective garment he had ever known how to wear.

Outside, the corridors were empty. And so was the gloaming elevator.

And that's just what made Charlie nervous.

The corporate pretense that nobody was around.

It was pretty hard not to notice Buster right away. Disguised in his old sailor outfit, he was still just about the only penguin in Times Square.

"Sort of thought I'd run into you out here," Buster said. He was paper-bagging a sixteen-ounce can of Bud and carrying his change of clothes in a lumpy white pillowcase. "I just don't see you doing the celebrity thing for too long, you know?"

"Fame is great—if you don't mind being somebody you don't want to be around," Charlie said. "Now come on, pal. Let's go find some place that isn't New York."

PART 6

THE WORLD OF WORK

1

DOWN SOUTH

Roy worked hard on a farm all day, and slept every night in a big barn with many moo-cows, horsies, and baa-baas. The moo-cows were Roy's favorite, especially the one named Elsie with the biggest udders. Whenever Roy found himself growing nostalgic about Wanda and the great sex they used to have together, he would begin looking at Elsie with a fondness that Elsie was too slow and cudulent to appreciate. The harder Roy stared, the better Elsie looked, until eventually Roy couldn't contain himself any longer. At this point he would climb over the wooden gate, grab roughly ahold of Elsie's wide, fly-bitten haunches, and give her a little of the old what for. It was quick and it was good. It even helped Roy forget about Wanda for a while.

Roy liked the South because it was hot, muggy, and littered with overripe fruits and vegetables. It was amazing the things you could find just walking down the road or through the fields on any given afternoon. Blackening figs, busted melons, sun-dried tomatoes, and rotting apricots were distributed freely across the hot dust like stray manna. All you had to do was tear off the smelly bits and toss them in your mouth. Insects, dust, road grease, and all.

Roy worked in the fields and ran errands for the plantation's top corporate management executives, Darrel and Chloe Johansen of the Georgia Plantation Counsel. The Counsel was a wholly owned subsidiary of the International Produce Board, which was itself an autonomous, self-sustaining division of, what else, Worldco Enterprises, Inc. Here the remote, unfriendly administrative staff spent their days hidden away in tartly air-conditioned offices, monitoring or being monitored by faceless account specialists and stock analysts from all over the Internet. They didn't mix with the farm staff. They didn't let their voices be heard over the loudspeakers. In fact, they didn't make any public appearances at all, unless it was to pose for photographers from the company's weekly newsmagazine, *At One With Worldco*.

Every evening after working up a healthy sweat lobbing spuds into a wooden barrel, Roy returned to his cot in the bunkhouse, popped a Bud, and leafed through the various disposable men's magazines and sports newsletters deployed as tablecloths in the Animal Mess. The pink, airbrushed human females were too clean and pink for Roy's tastes, but he loved browsing through the glossy advertisements for men's cologne, stereo equipment, and sports cars. Roy couldn't read, exactly, but he didn't need to.

"Buy a new car!" Roy improvised, running his fingers across the bold black letters and sounding out each imagined vowel, as if he were performing a sort of braille karaoke. "This car is really good! Drive this car and this blond girl will really love you! Buy this car and you will really love yourself!"

When his spud-roughened fingers reached the page's glossy bottom, Roy breathed a sigh of tremendous satisfaction. Reading, he decided, was easy. You didn't have to decipher what the figures meant. You only had to dream about who they wanted you to be.

Some nights, sated with glossy reading, Roy would wander around the barn talking out loud to himself and pretending Wanda had come back. He imagined preparing exotic meals of banana soup, banana stew, and banana cream pie, serving them to her on a candlelit picnic table in back of the barn while soft music played on his transistor radio. When Wanda came home, he would teach her how to love again. He would teach her about what slick magazines called "the new romance," and about what he called "the new Roy."

"You are looking very beautiful tonight, my dear," Roy would say out loud, pouring multiple glasses of chilled Gallo Tawny Port or lime-dashed Safeway Gin. "Have I told you about this little magazine article I was reading yesterday? It seems that this very beautiful young woman fell in love with a very beautiful young man because of his new underwear. How charming, you say? Oh yes, very charming, indeed."

The nights would pass in a long, slow rouse of passionate undress. Roy would satisfy Wanda in every conceivable orifice, and somewhere along the line she would satisfy him in every orifice, too. Fireworks, violins, crystal chandeliers, ballroom dancing, caviar, and pearls. Around them in the glowing, shaggy barn the assembled horsies and baa-baas would look on with blank, chewing amazement. They would wonder about this thing called Love. They would ask themselves, Why doesn't it ever happen to *me*?

Some nights Roy grew so drunk with washtub gin that he passed out in Elsie's stall, her inflated pink bloomers tangled around his ankles like an amorous receipt. When he awoke the following morning, the barn was shot through with shafts of moted sunlight. Outside, farm machinery revved and pigs bickered huskily over slop.

"Big night, Roy?" asked Tom Parkinson, the company overseer. Tom opened the gate to Elsie's stall and showed Roy a dented aluminum pail. "You hairy primitive types can't get enough of it, can you, boy?"

Roy sat up in the damp straw and reached for his sweaty forehead.

"I don't feel so good, Tom. I want to sleep some more. Could I please sleep some more, Tom? Or is it already time to get up?"

Tom Parkinson was a large, overexercised middle-management executive who had been kicked out of Worldco's New York office for either being too obsequious or not obsequious enough (even New Yorkers couldn't tell the difference these days).

He tossed Roy the dented aluminum pail with a hollow, blunt clattering.

"I don't think so, Roy," Tom Parkinson said, without a trace of sympathy. "You nailed Elsie, man. You milk her. And I'll expect this whole damn barn swept and dusted by oh-eight hundred hours. Or you can just *forget* about breakfast."

Roy loved the outdoor life, and looked back on the day he was parceled off to the free enterprise system as just about the best thing that had ever happened to him. Like Muzak in an elevator, life on the corporate farm constantly replayed an unending medley of Roy's favorite hits: porridge, sweat, sun-damaged fruit, televised sports in the Animal Canteen, and screwing Elsie the Cow like there was no tomorrow. Days turned into months, months into years, and Roy never once found himself being awkwardly surprised by things he'd never done, or experiences he'd never known.

Then, one day in late autumn, a strange new face appeared at the farm, and began to make Roy deeply uneasy about the only life he had ever lived.

"You guys are really pathetic, do you know that?" Dave the Otter had recently been appointed the statewide representative of Mr. Big's National Organization for Animals, which at last report was being run out of a P.O. box in the South Bronx. "You're sleeping in your own shit, for Christ's sake. You're drinking slime out of troughs. You're shuffling along saying 'Yes, Massah' and 'No, Massah' and 'Thanks for all the gruel, Massah,' while what're the corporate big shots doing? They're *laughing* at you guys, man. They're sitting up there in that big Bauhaus-like corporate monstrosity, sipping wine coolers behind their reflective windows and having a good old-fashioned hoot at all you stupid putzes down here. Working your butts off for *beans,* man. Being grateful for *slop.* "

Dave the Otter showed up in Roy's barn every evening after the final chow down. Standing behind a podium jury-rigged together from splintering orange crates and moldy lumber, he addressed the sparse crowd through a bottomless Big Gulp container that he wielded like a megaphone. Usually he began each Get Down Seminar by distributing a few tattered leaflets and questionnaires, or by playing an inspirational political announcement from Mr. Big.

"Ayaaanimooohls muuuuhsss yeeew-*nite!*" declared Mr. Big through the undependable medium of a Walgreen's-brand cassette player. "Pleeeeyuhz doooo-nate generuuuuuhshly tooo the caww-uhsh."

Then, after clicking off Mr. Big's Dopplering voice (which sounded as if it were being played on a bad high school film projector) Dave the Otter passed the hat while giving the animals their evening lesson in Intro to Animal Ec.

"What the boss's trying to say, see, is that you guys are like the manufacturers of wealth, and *you don't even know it,* man!" The most exciting thing about Dave the Otter was his ability to grow excited by his own rhetoric. It was an amazing, almost profound thing to watch, the barnyard denizens conceded. A fellow animal driven by the hard interior momentum of his own voice, and not by some spotty human being in a tractor. "You guys *work* the physical stuff that is the world, and there ain't nothing more important in the techno-capitalist system of wealth production. You guys till the soil. You guys lay the eggs. You guys express the milk and yogurt and cheese. You procreate, reduplicate, and rear your animal babies for human table fodder. You reach into the bowels of the earth and make food to eat, houses to live in, and clothes to wear. You guys enjoy what the boss calls 'an original and healthy relationship with worldly existence,' and that's a *good thing,* that's a *positive* thing. But what do those corporate big shots do all day, huh? While you guys are doing all the ball-breaking, heart-rending work of the world, what are those *people* doing in their air-conditioned cubicles, huh?"

Whenever Dave the Otter ventured a question, the crowd grew uneasy with itself. Cynical pigs smirked and swaggered in loose little circles. Moo-cows looked hammer-struck, dazed by their own inspeculation. Baa-baahs even stopped bleating and chewing, which were just about the only things they *knew* how to do. In fact, out of all the collective animal riffraff, only Roy, besotted by this point with cheap beer, made any effort at all to answer Dave's questions. Not because Roy thought the questions were important, but because he couldn't repress his lifelong desire to satisfy any animal who possessed more authority than he did.

"Are the human executive types working really hard, Dave?" Roy asked with a tiny belch. "I mean, erp, are they getting the food and clothes we make into grocery and department stores? And then do they look after us, and make sure we have enough food to eat and clothes to wear?"

Roy always liked the feel of the answer in his mouth, but he never liked the sound it made when it landed in the barn around him. It seemed to echo off the walls with an unraveling hiss.

"Distributing the wealth," Dave responded thinly. "Caring for you animals. Working really hard." Dave the Otter looked at Roy as if he were a big black hole in the middle of the barn. Somebody would have to fill that hole someday. Otherwise it would just sit there forever, resounding with its own absence.

"You're a real wizard, Roy, you really are." Dave shook his head slightly. "A really admirable hunk of animal intellect."

Roy breathed a sigh of relief. He liked when Dave understood how hard he tried—even if the majority of his answers were completely incorrect.

"Why, thank you, Dave," Roy said, saluting him with the potatoish dregs of his beer. "You're a pretty wizardly guy yourself."

2

MANHATTAN MELODY

Back in Manhattan, Roy's ex-wife, Wanda, was wishing Animal Activists would pack up all its rhetoric and go home. Everywhere she turned she saw urgent, half-familiar slogans scrawled on street-front walls and bus stop kiosks. Police sirens wailed in the congested streets, pursued by big white ambulances and pivoting Newswatch helicopters. Lone animals, adrift with shopping carts full of consumer refuse, were randomly hustled into police vans and crowd-control vehicles, while on the perimeters of every altercation louder, hastier animals shouted through staticky megaphones

"DON'T LET THIS HAPPEN TO YOU! DON'T LET THIS
HAPPEN TO YOU!"

before they were either surrounded by phalanxes of burly policemen, or else fled into the rapidly encroaching "bad neighborhoods."

There seemed to be a tremendous discord at work in the knotty medley of Manhattan, and Wanda didn't like it one bit. She didn't like the way she was leered at by passing taxi drivers, or the way she was refused seats in good restaurants and uptown movie theaters. But most of all she didn't like the way her custom was treated by the local merchants, as if they were doing her a big favor by taking her money.

"Nice day, isn't it, Habib?" Often, when Wanda tried to engage the corner grocer in friendly conversation, he didn't seem to like it. He hurled her fresh vegetables into a brown paper bag, and pushed her change back across the counter as if it was radioactive.

"No nice day," Habib told her, gesticulating rudely at the noisy streets outside. "Animals shitting everywhere, making noises about great country. Saying 'Humans bad,' 'Humans, go home,' 'Humans must die,' and other bad things. Habib come to this country and buy store, raise family, try to make great American country his home. I ask you, why can't animals do the same? Why can't animals realize how very lucky they are?"

Ever since Wanda's therapist, Dr. Reikoff, was taken into custody by the FBI, Wanda felt her entire life unraveling like cheap socks. Mrs. Garfield stopped appreciating her work in the kitchen, and Mr. Garfield stopped appreciating her work in the back hall. Joe the doorman stopped asking her out for late drinks at the Raccoon Lodge, and Barney the local cop on the beat stopped teasing her with a tip of his hat and a "Cheerio, Simba!" Worst of all, Wanda didn't have any of her old friends left to play with anymore. Whenever she called, she never got further than their scratchy answering machines.

"Oh hi, *Bobo?*"

Wanda leaned into the hall telephone, trying to evade the weird slurping sounds of the Garfields, who were currently in the dining room delving into Wanda's latest rendition of Moo-Shu Spicy Pork.

"I was just calling, that's all. Did you get any of my messages? Are you okay? When are we having Girls' Night Out again? Did you ever find a job? I can't seem to reach you anymore, Bobo. Not you and not Betty. Don't all these Animal Activists scare you a little? They sure scare me. Oh well."

Back in the dining room Stan Garfield erupted out of his own silence—which was the only way he knew to communicate anything these days.

"*Wanda!* Has this got *chili* in it! You know I can't eat chili on accounta my polyps!"

"Gotta go," Wanda whispered into the receiver, but it wasn't so easy hanging up. This thinly coiled plastic cord connected her to the only reality that still mattered. The one she couldn't get to. The one that wouldn't respond. "But call me back, will you? Promise? *Please?*"

But Wanda's friends never called back. And it began to look like they never would.

Then one day on her way home from picking up the children from school, Wanda passed a public demonstration. It was the first day of spring, and Wanda had been looking forward to this day all winter long.

"*Humans are bad! Animals are good! Humans are bad! Animals are good!*" This wasn't your usual ragtag shouting match, with a lot of cardboard bluster, but rather a mean, surly bunch of mismatched creatures that extended all the way across Park Avenue, blocking traffic for miles in every direction.

"What's everybody yelling about?" asked the Garfields' little girl. "Has there been an accident, Wanda? Where did all the police come from? Why are all those animals so angry?"

Wanda quickly hustled the children through a crowd of human onlookers. Many of the humans were dressed in business suits and carried briefcases. Others wore Levi's, brown headbands, tennis shoes, and packages of Marlboros rolled into the sleeves of their starched white T-shirts. There was something generic about their blue eyes and closely cropped blond hair, like packages in a budget supermarket.

"Just move along, children," Wanda told them. "Stop dawdling and move along." She was trying to interpose her body between them and the altercation of words in the street.

"Mr. Big *will* come! Mr. Big *will* come! Mr. Big *will* come!"

Then, as abrupt as a corner collision of yellow cabs, one of the generic blond types hurled a stone and the chanting divided up the middle into an arrhythmic beat.

"Mr. *Big. Will* come, Mr—*Come,* Mr. *Big. Will* come Mister Big—"

Then, from the crowd, another blond type turned beet red and shouted: "So go back to the woods, you creeps! You don't belong here! You don't *belong!*"

By the time Wanda had herded her miniature set of Garfields into their penthouse apartment, they were bubbling over with questions she didn't know how to answer.

"Why do people hate animals so much, Wanda?"

"Why do animals hate people?"

"Do you hate us, Wanda? Are we supposed to hate you?"

"Where'd those blond men get those neat armbands? Can you make me an armband? Can I wear one to school?"

And while Wanda boiled rice in a pot and arranged filleted chicken breasts on a baking sheet, she snapped and batted at the children's questions as if they were a swarm of stinging insects.

"No you *can't* wear an armband to school. I don't know why, you just can't. Animals *don't* hate people and *I* don't hate *you.* No, of course they'd never hurt you. They'd never hurt you because I wouldn't let them. No, *you* couldn't hurt *them,* either, and no, that doesn't mean I like *them* as much as I like *you.* Because it would be wrong, that's why. Because it wouldn't be *right!*"

With this Wanda would slam shut the oven door and activate the baking timer. Mr. and Mrs. Garfield were eating out tonight at a five-thousand-dollar-a-plate political rally for their favorite New York Senator, a former Republican who had recently joined the Democratic Party in order to help enact Republican legislation. (Wanda thought it was good for Mr. Garfield to get politically involved. After all, a man had to believe in *something*.)

The children blinked at one another in slow unison.

"But, Wanda, how do you know when something's wrong and when it's right? Don't all those people outside think *they're* right? And don't all those animals think *they're* right, too?"

This was the part Wanda hated. When their questions made more sense than her answers.

The only possible response she could come up with at such times was this: "Would you both *please* go into the living room and watch some TV. I've got work to do, remember?"

Then she disentangled their fingers from her hairy arms and sent them on their way.

3

TOP DRAWER

About this same time in Washington, D.C., the President of the United States was doing everything he could to catch up on world events.

"Yes, General. Yes, General. Yes, I *know* it's a jungle out there, General. No, just because it's covered with ice doesn't mean it's not a jungle. Of course not. Of *course* penguins are wild creatures, just like lions and tigers. Of course they can't be trusted. I'm not saying that, General. What I'm *trying* to say is— yes, General. Yes, of course, General. But that's what I'm trying to *tell* you, General. I *can't* send reinforcements, however much I'd—yes, General. Of course, General. Of course."

Sometimes the President had days like this. Here he was, the nation's Chief Executive Officer, and everybody treated him like some random voice on a 1-900 Complaint Line. Whatever happened to that good old American expression "When I say jump, you ask how high?" The only expression the President ever heard around the Oval Office anymore was "The buck stops here." Everything else was in Korean, Serbo-Croatian, or Japanese.

"Yes, General. I'm sure, General. Women are very fickle creatures, General, especially if you say so. Well, maybe she'll come back, General, maybe she's just taken a little— No, of course *I* wouldn't go to New York City for *my* holiday, either; I'd go bass fishing out on Lake— I'm sorry, General. Yes, you do matter to me. Bass fishing, yes, on Lake Winnemucca, but then I'm partial to— Yes, General. Yes. Of course I do. Yes. Yes, I do care about you personally, and not as a what? A randomly exploitable integer on the profit abacus of the multinational defense and weapons industry? No, absolutely not, General. You matter to me as an *individual human being.*"

The President twisted the receiver away from his mouth long enough to expel a long, pointless sigh. Meanwhile, the General's voice continued buzzing tinnily in the room like something out of Spin Control. Even when nobody was listening it still made a sound.

Then the front door opened and the President looked up.

"No, General, I don't want to put either you *or* your troops at the mercy of those, well, those penguins. And I'll personally okay your hiring of another native translator and personnel coordinator—and yes, General, yes, of *course* she can be female, of course she can. But I. Well I. No I. But, General. Yes, General. Okay yes."

Secretary of State Bill Murdley brought in the hot cocoa on an embossed silver tray and set it on the sea of varnished mahogany. He took the plush leather chair just to the President's left, and sank gently into their morning itinerary.

House Speaker, he read. Minority Whip. Finance Committee Chairman. The International Banking Spokesperson, the Fed Executive Committee, and last but not least, the business editor of *The New York Times.*

"But you hold the line out there, General. I said *hold the line.* No, General. No, I'm not *putting* you on hold—General? Hello? No, but I *do* have to go. And keep warm, will you? No, General, no, no, I've really *got* to go. Gotta go, General. No, I'll call *you,* General. Just try to have a nice time while you're down there—though of course I realize that'll be difficult. But really, General. Really. I'm not kidding this time. I've really gotta go."

As the President gently put down the receiver, he felt the entire Oval Office subside a little, like pistons in a deactivated combustion engine.

"Busy day, Mr. President?"

They both looked at the wall clock. It wasn't even 9:30 A.M.

"Busy day," the President conceded.

The President switched off the Call-In Request indicator, leaned back in his swivel chair, and propped his feet on the desk. He took the mug of hot cocoa to warm his palms, trying to make this moment last. This was far and away his favorite part about being President.

The President loved being briefed.

"We got problems, Mr. President." The Secretary of State noisily opened a manila folder in his lap. "Animal problems, Mr. President. Big ones."

The President sipped his hot cocoa and closed his eyes.

"Don't hesitate, man. Give it to me straight."

"What's that, Mr. President?"

The President smiled.

"Who is this Mr. Big," he asked. "And what the hell are we going to do about him."

On the President's lips they didn't sound like questions.

They sounded like answers about to happen.

PART 7

ADAPT, ADOPT, IMPROVE

1

OUT THERE AND IN HERE

They took the Bonanza bus from Grand Central to Waterbury, where they purchased a four-door convertible sedan at a corner used-car lot. The car lot was run by a shady Yankee entrepreneur named Joe.

"You from around here? You got bank references? You got a Connecticut driver's license?" Joe obviously didn't like the idea of Charlie taking his top-of-the-line lemon-mobile out for a test drive. His sunglasses were slate gray and humorless, making him look like either a hired thug or a cop.

"No," Charlie said, "but I got a fistful of Krugerrands," and pulled them out of his jacket pocket like dingy payola. "What do you think of that, huh? Does that make me an acceptable paying customer or what?"

They drove west that night with the wind. Tumbleweeds whipped past. Pale flapping newspapers, addled and radarless bats. The road quaked against their tires with a terrible inconstant rattle, making them suspect dark forces in the night—or perhaps just their lousy suspension.

Charlie drove and Buster rode shotgun. They watched the pocked lunar landscape slip past like studio montage in an old black-and-white movie.

"It's the one thing I can never take in," Charlie said, snapping off the dashboard radio and lighting a Tareyton. "America, the New World, Terra Incognita, all that vast and radiant grandeur *out there*. When Columbus arrived, he expected to find two-headed people, you know. Half-men and half-wolves. Creatures with faces for stomachs, multiple genitalia, gigantic winglike ears, and serpents for hair. Just look out there, Buster, look and *imagine*. All that space. All those places nobody's been."

Charlie activated the high beams with his left foot and the landscape brightened like a klieg-struck movie set. Shadows deepened and stars dimmed.

"Thousands of miles of it, Buster, in every direction at once. It's really a trip, man, like, flying over it? You never get used to just how much *isn't* out there."

They ate in roadside diners and visited many fabulous, over-priced monuments. Niagara Falls, Mt. Rushmore, Little Big Horn, the Alamo. It was Buster's first visit to America, and they were exploring it like he might never visit it again.

"I guess I've probably run away from just about every rela-tionship that's ever been important to me," Buster confessed one night over his customary banana-bacon cheeseburger and fries. "What makes me do it, huh, Charlie? I mean, Muk Luk's a nice girl and all. It's just she makes me feel so goddamn *guilty* all the time. Because I don't love her. Or I don't love her enough. Or I'm not with her enough. Or I'm not with her enough when I *am* with her, if you catch my drift. And when you get right down to it, Charlie, I didn't not-love Muk Luk because of her looks. In fact, I don't care what anybody says. In penguin terms, actually, Muk Luk doesn't look half-bad."

They were sitting in a faded booth behind the disconnected jukebox. The vinyl seats were cut and torn, exuding stained yellow padding.

"I'm afraid interpersonal animal relationships aren't really my strong suit, Buster," Charlie conceded, stirring Cremora into his oily coffee. He was trying to disregard the elderly waitress behind the counter, who was giving him mean looks about the generous tip she didn't expect to receive. "I mean, I never quite stuck around anyplace long enough to *have* a relationship. Certainly not one worth running away from, anyway."

Buster had to think about this for a minute.

"Have you never been in love, Charlie? Have you never even thought about it? I'm not saying you *should* think about it or anything, because it's pretty much the biggest hole of grief you could possibly dig for yourself. But despite all that, well, I don't know, there's something to it in the long run. If only I could stick around long enough to figure out what that important something was."

Back in New York, Muk Luk wasn't sleeping and couldn't keep down solid foods. She suffered from headaches, nausea, dizziness, and irritable bowels. She couldn't even watch TV anymore, or go channel surfing via remote control. All she could think about was him. Him with that evasive little glint in his eyes. Him anointed with the aroma of fresh mackerel. Him with his streamlined shoulders and webbed, thorny feet. With Buster gone, nothing mattered anymore. Muk Luk just lay around all day waiting for maid service to lift her out of the way of the latest fresh sheets.

"You'll find someone else," Rick tried to console her, extracting the depleted mug of Stolichnaya from her hairy fist. "One morning, bingo, you'll wake up and it'll happen—you'll fall in love all over again. I mean, things could be a lot worse, right? We could be back there sleeping with the popsicles, babe. We could be scraping frost off our eyeballs and icicles off our toes."

Muk Luk was sitting up in her wide brass bed and staring at the overhead chandelier. A million points of refracted light. And in none of them would she see Buster ever again.

"Muk Luk wouldn't mind," she said dully, like aluminum hangers chiming in an empty closet. "New York City too fast for Muk Luk. Muk Luk want to stop hurting so much."

All night she lay awake and wondered, and all day she lay awake and dreamed. Room service, fed by direct access to Charlie's fat royalty accounts, provided her every commodifiable indulgence: caviar, french toast, closed-circuit pornography, and Courvoisier. Yet Muk Luk's senses were never satisfied, her expectations never fulfilled. Everywhere she looked the world was packed with absence and indeterminacy. How? Why? When? Who cares? And by repeatedly asking herself these same blunt, dull questions, Muk Luk learned two frightening things right away.

The answers were everywhere.

And they didn't mean anything to her anymore.

2

PRIVATE LIFE IN PUBLIC PLACES

High in the humming, air-conditioned offices of Worldco, head honchos from all over the corporate Internet were gathering to discuss the precipitately perilous world situation.

"Charlie the Crow's sales potential has peaked and then some, boy!" expostulated Ray from Marketing. "Sales are down. Merchandising orders are down. Spirits are down. Retail endorsement, product placement opportunities, crossover potential—all down down down. I've got a warehouse full of Charlie the Crow pot warmers and oven mitts and I can't *give* them away, Jesus. And the *returns*. Not in your blackest nightmares, man. They're coming back in drove. Big fat convoys of buses and eighteen-wheelers. Bulky gray sacks from the post office, certified-return and C.O.D. It's like a total bummer, man. It's like I can't believe what I'm doing here, you know? I used to have *ideals,* man. I was at Kent State. I was at Woodstock. I used to groove to Melanie, dig? And like now my wife and I? We hardly even do it anymore. I'm thinking of giving up entirely and going back to school. Maybe get another degree or something, who knows. Maybe even study English Literature. I used to really love English Literature—William Blake, and Wordsworth, and all those guys? But these days I get home about nine or ten and I'm so tired I can't even piss straight. So I just watch Letterman, or *Studs,* or something like that, and take a sleeping pill. What's happening to our world, man? What's happening to the world we used to know and love?"

Someone called Security and, before anybody knew it, Ray from Marketing was being heavily sedated and carried out on his shield. And nobody batted an eye in the big, massy Blue Room of Worldco International.

Corporate directors, marketing and sales administrators, legal henchmen, and token henchwomen sat around the long flat mahogany table with a sort of inauspicious bluster, as if they were waiting for a chauffeur to take them somewhere else *really* important.

"So much for today's Marketing report," said the CEO with a dry, almost contrite punctuality. The CEO projected the attitude that he was either incredibly important or totally innocuous—

even he wasn't sure which. "Now let's turn to Bart from Product Development, and find out what's happening in the more creative regions of our organization. Bart?"

The wide cool boardroom was thick with dead, machinery-manufactured air. A few individuals cleared their throats. The silence was so immense that many of them couldn't help hearing all that nonsilence verging outside.

Us, cried something out there in the streets. *Us. Us. Us. Us.*

"Well," Bart interjected, "so far as the creative end, I guess we just, you know, ahem, move on, right? New ideas. New products. New sales forces. New notions of how retail outlets should be owned and operated. And as far as, you know, the *creative* end, well, let me introduce you all to our new Creative Management Counseling Administrator, whom we've just brought in from one of our, er, *sister* companies. Bunny? Would you like to say a few words?"

Bunny Fairchild was leaning one elbow against the table while she perused the long line of mostly male honchos. Bunny was thinking, I used to make coffee for these guys. I used to fend off their muggy advances and endure their stupid posturing. And just look—now it's *their* turn to wait for *moi.*

The silence was sweet. But it didn't last long.

("Us. Us. Us. Us . . .")

Bunny passed out the uniform manila folders. Then she turned to Bobby, her personal administrative assistant, and whispered a few sharp words.

Causing Bobby to excuse himself, walk around the long table, and exit crisply through the tall gleaming doors.

"If you'll open your folders, gentlemen, we can take a look at some ideas I've been developing recently."

There was the bright rasp of papers while a sigh of contentment reached through the entire building. The board members loved Bunny because she was the perfect commercial product representative. She never asked them what they wanted, but only told them what to buy.

The tall doors opened again and Bobby reentered, accompanied by a chorus line of grizzly, deodorant-scented animals dressed in formal evening attire.

The animals shuffled nervously in awkward shoes, conferring among themselves while trying to toe the almost imperceptible chalk line. Bobby helped them find their places.

"As you all know," Bunny continued, "our Charlie the Crow merchandising campaign has reached saturation levels, so it's time to move on to greener pastures. In other words—we're looking for animals. Cute fuzzy animals. Animals with personality. Animals who don't play by the rules, but animals who won't cause us any trouble, either. I'm talking a Bruce Willis kind of animal, but without the sexual dynamics. I'm talking Madonna, but without the lawyers. Now, if you'll take a look at the animals I've assembled here today, I think you'll find yourselves confronted by a wealth of genuine, forward-looking nonhumanoid talent. So let me see . . ."

Bunny consulted her manila folder.

"Animal number seven? Would you step forward, please?"

The animals shuffled and murmured among themselves, trying to read the numbered tag cards each wore around his or her neck. Eventually, way down at the end of the line, Animal #7 took a brief, exploratory step forward.

Bunny turned to the top fact sheet in her folder. Then she began to read out loud.

"Gorilla, Wanda Phillipa. Born: August 30, 1963. Birthplace: Darkest Africa. Birth Sign: Leo. Eyes black, hair black. Personality profile: sensitive, bawdy, fun to be around, eager to please. Wanda's wearing a floor-length sequined ball gown by Givenchy. Her hair has been permed by Sassoon, her nails sculpted by Bloomie's. I don't know if this is *exactly* the style of presentation we want to take with Wanda, but I thought we could kick it around for a while and see who scores the first goal. Primarily I'm thinking in terms of fun libido. Sexy, but with a sense of humor about herself. Kind of like Zsa Zsa *used* to be . . . So, Wanda? Is there anything you'd like to say to the nice gentlemen assembled here today?"

"Well, I don't know, I guess."

Deep beneath her matted fur, Wanda blushed. Thickly draped in Givenchy she felt weirdly naked, as if the laws of social decorum had been inverted by the dizzying parameters of this large, underdecorated boardroom.

"I guess I love New York, I guess."

All around the massive table, the board members smiled. They were thinking about their homes in the country, automatic lawn sprinklers, and young German au pairs with dusky red lips.

"And I like nice clothes, I guess. And romance, probably. And being taken out to really nice restaurants. Though usually my boyfriend, Stan, he likes to eat in."

The board members continued to smile.

"And I like to have a good time, and work hard. And I guess I think of myself as a positive-minded individual, you know, in that I'm not overly critical about things? You know, like all those noisy demonstrators outside, who don't have any *positive* things to say about our country, but can only criticize everything and tear it down? Maybe that doesn't make me very political or something, but I don't know, I still *think* of myself as political. I mean, I always try to be good to my friends, and do the right thing and so on. In the end, though, I guess I just want to be happy, and meet new people, and find a decent apartment and, you know, maybe even fall in love someday. I don't think that's asking too much, is it?"

"Thank you, Wanda."

Bunny turned Wanda's fact sheet face down on the mahogany desk and Wanda abruptly ceased to be or mean, as if some sort of existential switch had been thrown.

A long moment occurred that passed for silence.

("Us. Us. Us. Us.")

"Animal number fourteen?" Bunny silently directed the other board members to turn to the next fact sheet. At least one board member muttered out loud, "I really dig that crazy Wanda-chick."

Undeterred, Bunny continued.

"Alaskan Husky, Rick. Born: March 6, 1989. Birthplace: Nome, Alaska, but transferred with his family to Antarctica while still a pup. Birth sign: Pisces. Personality profile: Loyal to a fault. Loves to chase sticks and balls. Exceptionally handsome and rugged, with first-glance appeal to both young girls and boys. Today Rick's wearing a studded leather collar from Frederick's of Hollywood. I thought with Rick we'd shoot for good old-fashioned mute American heroism—never goes out of fashion, right? A really good dog who saves human beings from every conceivable disaster. Fires, floods, famines, etcetera. Of course, we'll need to start breeding a race of stunt dogs and body doubles for the action shots, but I don't think old Rick'll mind. What do you say, Rick? Are you willing to be loaned out to stud, big boy?"

"Sounds cool," Rick panted happily. Rick liked being in a roomful of mostly male human beings, since he figured the odds were pretty solid that at least *one* of them had a really good stick to throw.

"Rick?" Bunny inquired formally. "Is there anything *you'd* like to tell us about yourself?"

Rick began to drool.

"Yeah," he said. "I guess I could go for a really big bowl of water about now."

With a flick of her eyes and a miniature beep from her digital watch, Bunny turned the next page. And Rick joined Wanda in the realm of the postexistent.

"Eskimo, Muk Luk," Bunny read out loud. "Born: April 27, 1955. Birthplace: Somewhere in Alaska. Now, as most of you guys have already noticed, Muk Luk isn't exactly an animal, but then she isn't much of a human being, either. I thought we could go for a sort of primitive mystery with Muk Luk. Muk Luk's tough, but that doesn't mean she isn't loving, too. With Muk Luk, by the way, we're presented with a terrific opportunity for what I call associational glow. This means Muk Luk's former connection with Charlie will lend us commercial momentum from the previous campaign, but without us having to take any responsibility for it. In other words, the public doesn't know Muk Luk yet, but they think that they *should*. In fact, on this point alone I'm pretty high on the Eskimo idea. Except for one small thing."

But it was already perfectly obvious to everybody.

"The face," Bunny said.

A few tears dribbled from underneath Muk Luk's freckled eyelids and unfurled into her furry cheeks.

"Animal number nineteen . . ." Bunny said after a while. "Animal number thirty-four . . . Animal number twelve . . . Animal number forty-five . . ."

The long afternoon waned. Outside, the voices were growing louder. And the louder they got, the more intensely the corporate honchos pretended not to hear.

While the animals counted off, the CEO browsed listlessly through the latest issue of *USA Today,* his favorite newspaper of all time. He especially liked the color-coded graphs and statistical charts, the thick margins and user-friendly op-ed page. Best of all, though, he liked the way it presented itself on every street corner like a TV program. Screw the Germans and the Japs, the CEO often reflected. They may have manufacturing, but *we've* got *packaging.*

"Animal number twenty-seven," Bunny said. "Animal number three . . . Animal number twenty-one . . . Animal number nine . . ."

At the bottom of page two's gossip column sat a photograph of Mr. Big wearing a black hood over his face. Two eyeholes were clipped out, as were two additional passages for his knobby horns. Mr. Big had spoken in Harlem last weekend, and was scheduled to speak in Central Park later that afternoon. In this standard publicity photo, he stood flanked by a pair of burly Dobermans wearing armbands and bandilleros.

Now *that's* the sort of animal we need on *our* side, the CEO thought. Someone with a little moxie. Someone like Mr. Big.

"Animal number forty," Bunny said. She could feel the corporate attention starting to wander. Which was why she always saved the best for last.

The next animal stepped forward, wearing something silky and revealing over the bottom half of her body, and something shiny and chic over the top half. Her outfit resembled a cross between French lingerie and a skindiver's wet suit.

A brief *ahem* ignited the assembled gentlemen.

The interview was already well under way.

"And what do you do, Sandy? In Antarctica, I mean?"

"Well, I used to be a housewife, but then after the invasion . . . I mean, the *liberation,* I got an office job with the General, and, well, one thing led to another, you know."

"No, Sandy, I *don't* know. Why don't you try to explain?"

"Well, I was eventually assigned as General Heathcliff's personal assistant. This means I handled his social calendar, and helped him entertain foreign dignitaries, and kept the quarters tidy, and so on. Sometimes I acted as the General's personal envoy, sort of, well, *escorting* VIPs to and from their Antarctic destinations. In fact, that's why I was at JFK when some of your scouts 'discovered' me for this audition. I was acting as liaison for these two officers here, and we'd just flown in together on Air Tundra."

Bunny felt a slight jar of discontinuity invade the room, as if someone had let in too much fresh air. She looked all the way down to the front of the long animal line, where Wanda sat splay legged on the floor, picking her feet. Then her eyes roamed back up the line and past Sandy again until they landed on the two strangest animal creatures in the entire building.

"Excuse me, fellas." Bunny's voice could have frosted windows. "Can I help you?"

One of the men was bruised, tall, muscular, and wore green military fatigues. Next to him stood a humanoid figure wrapped from head to foot in white puffy bandages. Both wore Kalishnikov rifles over their shoulders, and had trouble standing at attention because of their various splints and plaster casts.

"Lieutenant Colonel Jack Hollister, at your service, ma'am." The Lieutenant Colonel performed a mock half-salute, which was about as far as his right arm extended anymore. "And this is my partner, Sergeant Yuri Rudityev from Foreign Exchange." He turned to the bandaged humanoid. "Say something to the lady, Yuri."

"Glig duh bluffy diggy-buds," Yuri shouted, his volume and articulacy muffled by multilayered cotton and gauze. "Glig duh bluffy diggy-buds!"

Bunny passed her disbelief up and down the boardroom table, but nobody examined it too closely. The collective board members were trying to gauge the true, heartfelt opinions of their bulky CEO, who was snoring faintly into a pillow of brightly colored newspapers.

"The General suggested we might work together, Ma'am," Hollister said. "We read about the bounty you offered through *Manhunt Monthly* and got here as soon as we could."

Hollister unscrolled the magazine from his back pocket to display a slick page-length advertisement. The advertisement read:

WANTED: DEAD OR ALIVE

CHARLIE THE CROW

FOR BETRAYING THE TRUST OF THE AMERICAN PEOPLE

(GIVE US HIS HEAD ON A STICK AND WE'LL GIVE YOU $100,000)

[This offer not valid in Puerto Rico, Canada, or the Philippines.]

Everyone in the room exchanged a rapid semaphore of meaningless glances with everybody else. Outside, the terrible silence continued to speak: "Us. Us. Us. Us."

Then, as if aggravated by inattention, the severely bandaged humanoid beside Hollister began squirming with barely restrainable forces.

"Glig duh bluffy diggy-buds!" His shouting threatened to burst forth from his bandages like a terrible butterfly. "Glig duh bluffy diggy-buds!"

Suddenly, Bunny felt strangely calm. The professional tension ebbed from her body in an uncustomary catharsis.

The world, she thought, is actually crazier than I am.

"What's with your friend?" she asked Hollister, as if he was the only other person in the entire building. "What's he trying to say?"

Hollister smiled at her and thought, Too skinny. Not enough meat.

"He's saying 'Kill the bloody dickie-birds. Kill the bloody dickie-birds. Kill the bloody dickie-birds—' "

"I get the picture," Bunny said.

But nice boobs, Hollister added to himself.

It was his turn to speak.

"I hope so, lady," he said. "Because this time we're not on military orders or anything. This time it's fucking personal."

PART 8

THE REVENGE OF NATURE

1

POP STAR

It wasn't even a political crisis anymore. It was a crisis of repre-
sentation, and that was the scary part. Words no longer represented things, governments no longer represented people, and
images no longer represented stuff. All across Animal Planet, animals were giving up on rhetoric altogether. Instead they were
taking up big sticks, rocks, broken bottles, axe handles, splintery pool cues, and two-by-fours.

Animals stormed Parliament, Congress, the Bastille, Moscow,
and Beijing. They detonated barns, henhouses, trash barrels,
birdbaths, army jeeps, and laundry hampers. The streets boiled
over with wild rabbits, itinerant geese, subversive antelope, radical yaks, freedom-crazed dingoes, and politically correct pigs.
All across the planet animals raged and swore and ruined and
trampled. They brayed and woofed and snorted and chirped.

"We are not animals!" Mr. Big roared through a whistling lapel
microphone one afternoon in Central Park. "We are goodness!
We are justice! We are might! We are right! And we will *not* wait
forever, not another *minute* or another *second!* Because we want

it *now!* We want it *now!* We want it *now!* We want it *NOW!*"

Mr. Big was clopping back and forth on the polished wooden podium, wearing the customary black hood over his widely antlered head. He was drenched with sweat and libido like James Brown after an especially salty rendition of "Soul Man."

Then, with a mighty swirl of his glimmering black robe, Mr. Big came to a halt at the exact dead center of the platform. And turned to confront the stunned and awestruck multitudes.

"So what are we waiting for, my fellow beasties? Will it be *their* world forever? Or will it be *our* world *tonight?*"

As Mr. Big was hurried from the stage by a pair of armed body-guards, revenge-crazed animals went charging off in every direction. They flattened bushes, hotdog stands, fences, benches, even small trees and trash cans. Their combined roar shook the pebbles in the earth and the leaves in the trees. Their day had come. And they were living it like it might never come again.

"Great going, boss," chattered Dave the Otter, leading Mr. Big down a flight of rickety wooden stairs to the basement dressing room. "Greatest speech of your life, I swear. You really know how to turn a phrase, boss. You really know how to make those crazy animals *listen.*"

Mr. Big was tired, enervated, and a little sad. All those waiting faces out there, waiting for his voice, his hopes, his dreams. They weren't even his anymore; they were *theirs.* His dreams belonged to *them.*

The two large orangutans bullied through the dressing room while Mr. Big stood panting outside. They threw open closets and cupboards with a pale, nasty vigilance, wearing armbands and shoulder-holstered Mausers. Once assured that the room was clear, they returned outside and took their stations on both sides of the door.

Mr. Big entered the dressing room, and Dave the Otter wasn't far behind.

"It was like the Sermon on the Mount, boss. It was like Hendrix at Woodstock, or that Ross Perot fellah on TV. I especially liked that part about the responsibilities of dreaming. That was really, you know, like *poignant?* Poignant as hell, boss. It really was."

Mr. Big trotted to the bureau and pulled off his stiff white collar, his robe, and his boots. Looking up he confronted his own hooded reflection in a tall thin dressing mirror. It wasn't even his reflection anymore. It, too, belonged to *them.*

Dave the Otter was chain-smoking Marlboros and riding the crest of a brisk nicotine buzz.

"And that part about going up in the spaceship, boss? Seeing the whole planet, man, the whole beautiful planet laid out below us? And like, what did you say? Like we've all got to decide, man, if we want to be part of this big beautiful planet or not? Why, that was more than *poignant,* man. That was, man, that was *inspired.*"

Mr. Big observed his hooded reflection with something less than grandeur. He was a very large animal, that was true. He was strong, powerful, and awesomely fecund—quite a potent stud in his younger days. But now he hardly recognized himself. In fact, he looked more familiar to himself with the hood on than with it off.

"I stole it from a bird," Mr. Big said. He leaned back until his rough haunches found the cream-colored sofa-chair. The chair was worn through in places, exposing patches of cheesy foam. It was Mr. Big's favorite recreational device, and he ritually transported it to the site of every stage performance, from Tokyo to Bhopal.

"His name was Charlie," Mr. Big said, "and he was a very powerful speaker in his time. He was a liar, though, who lied for all the wrong reasons. To make himself feel important. To get media attention. To hear himself talk. I, on the other hand, am Mr. Big, and I lie for all the *right* reasons. Because I am out to save all animals, regardless of gender or species."

Dave the Otter took a series of rapid puffs, as if he were trying to get a good blaze going on the tip of his cigarette.

"Absolutely, boss. Nobody doubts your integrity in the slightest. Did you see that crowd take off, man? Savage in tooth and claw, boy. I wish I could see them now."

Somewhere in the distance, a singular wild animal roared.

"Fifth Avenue," Mr. Big said, without intensity or conviction.

With a slow-rolling motion of his shoulders, Mr. Big leaned against the hat rack and snagged the tip of his white hood on one of its brass hooks. Then, as if he were pulling himself gently out of a hot bath, he slipped the hood from his head and confronted his own hard, diurnal reflection in the shimmery mirror.

The reflection that would always be his.

No matter how loudly the crowds screamed for more.

Dave the Otter had been kept pretty busy since the corporate takeover of Dave's Trading Post. Tossed out on his asset-stripped duff by the joint stockholders of Worldco, Military Supply Factory Outlets, and the Gap, Dave had eventually found himself somewhere in Brazil, suffering from partial memory loss, half a bottle of bad rum, and a porker-nymphomaniac named Stella. It had been a disastrous comedown. Once: prosperity, riches, a sense of self-worth. Now: a sudden basement flat in the *barrio*, no food in the cupboards, and Stella's faint aroma of musky sausage pervading the bathroom's shower curta.ins. Suddenly

Dave had lost everything he once held dear. He didn't even have his old self-esteem left to keep warm.

He needed truth and he found it fast. *Mr. Big Speaks,* distributed free on street corners and in public laundromats. It kept his mind diverted from itself. Someday, he promised, he would teach them all. With Mr. Big's help, he would teach the whole planet.

"What would I have done without you, boss? Where would I have gone? I wouldn't have nothing left to believe in, would I?"

Dave was scrubbing Scaramangus's back with a stiff-bristled brush and a pint of Walgreen's Baby Shampoo. It was the morning after the Manhattan conflagration and they were sharing a local stable with a pair of disgruntled old nags named Asphodel and Roger. Overhead, large clouds of smoke drifted back and forth with the breeze. The city was amazingly silent. Not even the leaves whispered. Not even the stones.

"Pop that blister," Scaramangus intoned, indicating a ripe carbuncle on his shoulder. "And more fragrances, Otter. More perfumes and conditioners."

"Sure, Boss. Whatever you say." Dave the Otter found the carbuncle between his paws and gave it a terrific squeeze. A plug of white fat burst, missing Dave's left eyeball by inches. Puss oozed from the sore, and Dave swiped it with his brush. "It's a brand new day, ain't it, Boss? Kind of like redemption, only *we* made it for *ourselves,* right, Boss? Not some phoney-baloney God or Savior. From now on, *we're* responsible for our own lives. And we've got nobody left to blame anymore but *ourselves.*"

News was sporadic from the streets. According to rumor, most of Manhattan was now utterly subdued. The zoos and kennels had been busted open, their inmates freed. Animals occupied local council offices, finance centers, libraries, and communications networks. Hunkered down in distant, smoldering buildings, Mr. Big's starry-eyed brethren were unreachable by phone, fax, or public conveyance. And as for human beings, there were none at all still visible on the streets. None left alive, that is.

"The Day of Atonement is not supposed to be easy," Mr. Big said. He was gazing up into the bright blue sky. The air crisp, the trees tall. Here at the center of the storm, everything was tranquil, like a surgical patient under heavy sedation. "Tomorrow we will rise from the ashes and build a New World Order. We will receive our dispensation from the flames. And we will build again, my fellow beasties. We will build again."

Mr. Big's voice incited Dave to brush harder and more briskly. He scrubbed so hard that the pores of Mr. Big's skin welled with blood.

This, Dave knew, was just the way Mr. Big wanted it. To be loved so hard it hurt.

"That's right, Boss. The Final Dispensation. The New World Order. It's already here, Boss. It's already here."

Nearby in their stables, the two white-haired nags shuffled uneasily, trying to keep warm in all the cold rhetoric blowing around.

"Maybe they're right," muttered shaggy Asphodel to her mate. "Maybe the world *has* changed for the better. Maybe for the first time in our lives it finally *is* safe to live among the animals."

But Roger, tamping his chipped right hoof against the ground to count out old memories, was not convinced.

"It will never be safe to live among the animals," he replied. "Because animals will always be animals. And meat will always be meat."

2

FAST TRACK

As per usual, Rick the Husky was the last animal to figure out what was going on, and the first to do anything about it.

"We need a car," he told the others. "We need provisions, camping supplies, citizen's band, and petrol." He was hustling the others down the thinly carpeted corridors like a sheepdog herding lambs into a pen. Fire alarms were shrieking while overhead extinguishers spewed forth streams of white water. "We've got to remain calm, rational and focused, because there are only two important things to worry about right now. Taking care of our own, and covering our asses."

All around them corporate employees were running for their lives. Secretaries, personal assistants, management training coordinators, investment counseling administrators, marketing research facilitators, executive salary watchdogs, stock portfolio analysts, and counseling-advisory technicians. They were either trampling one another like fire-wrought cattle in a pen, or stealing everything that wasn't nailed down.

Rick the Husky hurried his friends through the abrupt red door of an Emergency Exit, where they confronted an impossible labyrinth of stairwells, grown men weeping, and shredded memos flung everywhere like some last-minute obfuscation. The demonstrators had even infiltrated the subbasement parking garage, where they were overturning Volvos and urinating everywhere. Occasionally they grabbed a fleeing corporate employee and tore him or her limb from limb. Amidst the flickering fluorescents, the cold gray concrete was spattered with hunks of dead meat, rended cotton-blend sports jackets, and hastily discarded mace canisters like some poorly monitored abattoir.

Rick hustled Wanda and Muk Luk into a four-wheel-drive vehicle with keys. It started right up.

Damn, Rick thought. Those Japs sure know how to make cars.

New York City was vast, blazing, and Biblical with conflagrations. Gigantic birds swooped down from the sky, fat rats scampered out of sewers, and everywhere fleeing humans were pursued by gangs of wild beasts. We don't want *you,* the animals cried as they pulled down another lawyer, or another middle-management executive, or another over-financed political lobbyist. We don't want *you,* or *you,* or *you.* Carnage was everywhere, with plenty of fleeing humans to go around. Chomp, mutilate, savage, tear. At this rate, it would be years before the animals got around to turning on one another.

Rick the Husky took them out via the FDR, over the Triborough, and across the rocky Bruckner. The road was pitted and slagged with tar like the aftermath of some volcanic explosion.

"It looks like the end of the world," Wanda said, huddled in the backseat, her Givenchy sequined ball gown pulled up around her waist like the leaves of some gigantic, lewd lettuce. It looks like the Final Judgement. It looks like *Panic in the Year Zero.*"

Rick the Husky drove while smoking a Marlboro, and Muk Luk sat in the passenger seat with her spear propped between her legs.

"Just look at this dump, man," Rick said. "How can human beings endure it, huh? This isn't a community. It's a *state of siege.*"

"City without hope," Muk Luk said. "City without love. City without a lot of things. But most of all, city without Buster." Then she started crying into the matted collar of her undersanitized snow parka. Muk Luk didn't care about revolutions, urban-enterprise zones, public schools, disintegrating infrastructures, or even the wide dark horizon of fat geographical space *out there*. All she knew anymore was her own internal vacancy. It was rapidly becoming the only thing she wanted to know.

"No more deli sandwiches," Wanda said sadly. She peered through the rear window at the blazing city, but saw only the inverted reflection of her own hairy, mournful face. "No more matinees at the Ziegfeld. No more Macy's. No more Bloomie's."

Wanda could vaguely discern the buttresses of intersecting freeways, bridges, and offramps. Looming billboards promoted call-in numbers for Sex Talk, Psychic Love, and Cop Killer Info.

"I miss my kids," Wanda concluded mournfully. "I even miss my awful husband, Roy the Gorilla."

They could hear the sirens. They could see vast blocks of flickering electricity. They could smell smoke, creosote, and gasoline. Rick the Husky kept glancing suspiciously in the rearview mirror. He simply couldn't figure.

Why wasn't anybody on the freeway but them?

"Lots of people may criticize New York," Wanda explained softly, wiping a slender tear from one eye. "But you never see anybody in a big hurry to leave."

3

THE BIG BRIEFING

Within the hour the President and his top security advisors were conferring in the White House's basement screening room. In addition to the same old NSC people, the Secretary of State had assembled a number of new faces, plenty of hot coffee, and a shrimp-buffet lunch for two hundred.

"You remember Bob Ryerson, don't you, Mr. President. Assistant Security Director of Special Forces in London."

"Mr. President."

"And John Stout, our Media Consultant on International Animal Relations."

"Mr. President."

"And of course the Attorney General's Staff Secretary, Adrienne Velikovsky, who'll be standing in for her superior this morning. Seems the Attorney General's booked a gig promoting her new book later today on *Oprah*."

"Mr. President."

"And this is Ryerson's personal assistant, Becky Sanvoy, who made that great marshmallow salad for the last Presidential soirée at Downing Street. If you remember."

"Mr. President."

"And these are the Sanchez Brothers, former Special Missions Operators for that last aborted Cuba project."

"Señore el Presidente."

"Señore el Presidente."

"And this is—Christ, is that you, Manuel? This is, I'm sorry, Mr. President, there's been a mix-up in the screening procedures. This is Manuel, the pool boy."

"Mr. President. There's a serious chlorine problem in the White House."

"Let's tackle that chlorine problem later, okay, Manuel? And over here, Mr. President, is our CIA Research Coordinator, Roger Arnoldson. Rog used to work for UPI before coming over to our side. He's part of the improved relations we've been forging with our better halves over there in the fifth estate. Rog?"

"Morning, Mr. President. Big problems brewing out there in Animal Land, and I respectfully suggest that we get onto them right away. *While* there's still time."

"Rog wrote, produced, and directed the docu-brief we'll be

watching in just a few moments, Mr. President. But first, anybody for a quick sandwich or coleslaw? Feel free to eat during the screening, but keep down the slurping noises, okay? And please, *no talking*. I hate *talking* when I'm trying to watch a movie."

With as little ceremony as possible, the President took his special seat in back of the room, raised above all the others in a plush leather-bound sofa-chair. He liked to see the backs of all those assembled heads laid out beneath him like bowling pins in his own private alley.

The Secretary of State was holding a large icy Coke in one hand and a lined yellow legal pad in the other.

"Roll it, Sid!" he shouted.

The projector's engine activated with a tiny kick and a whir. White light splashed the screen, flickering until a frame of color caught.

4

3

2

1

Tum-tah-tah-taaah!

The National Security Council
Supported by Federally Approved Grants
From the National Aerodynamics and Space Administration,
Coca Cola,
C.I.A. Covert Domestic Operations
and the Ford Motor Corporation
Proudly Present—

Tum-tah-tah-taaaah!

A Roger Arnoldson Production
of a Roger Arnoldson Film
WARNING AMERICA:
THE MR. BIG SYNDROME

Tum-tah-tah-taaaah!

In the darkened auditorium, the audience members were already fidgeting in their chairs.

Like one of the President's own public addresses, this was the sort of briefing that could go on *forever.*

4

ETHNOCENTRISM

General Heathcliff, flanked by two anxious adjutants, was fleeing north by starlight, pursued by howling penguins armed with overpriced U.S. weaponry. During his entire tour of duty in Antarctica, it was probably the only time the General had ever ventured outside the Officers' Quarters, and he kept thinking it wasn't quite as cold as he'd expected out here. He'd certainly never seen so many stars.

"Some animals just don't know what's good for them," General Heathcliff explained as he slogged and slid across the plain of ice in his regulation green fatigue army boots. In the rear distance he could discern a tribe of small black-and-white dots, breaking apart and reforming into weirdly pointillist patterns. He could hear the *pop pop pop* of inadequately serviced M15s being fired in his general direction. "They think that power's something they *want,* for chrissake. Power over their environment, power over themselves. They think freedom's something more than just another big fat responsibility, and simply don't understand what a God-almighty drag it is most of the time. All the sleepless, lonely nights. All the unrequited passion and bad checks. I busted my balls for those birds, and what thanks do I get? A few cans of K rations and a secondhand down parka. Balls, I say. Big fat feathery penguin *balls!*"

"Just another mile or so, General," his adjutants implored. "If we can just make those mountains, sir, we'll be okay. We'll live to fight another day."

"Balls to the fight, I say!" The General tromped his exclamations into the hard ice like declarations of principle. "Let the bastards *keep* Penguin Island, for all I care! Let *them* fix the streetlights, build the malls, issue the proclamations, hear the endless fucking complaining! 'We don't like the curfew, General Heathcliff! We don't like paying taxes! We don't like this, General, and we don't like that.' I've never heard so much bloody whining in my entire life! If penguins are ready to take care of themselves, well, good riddance—that's what I say. Because they certainly won't have General Anthony Heathcliff to kick around any longer! And that's for *damn* sure!"

They tracked down the General at the steps of Mount Erebus, bound him up with packing tape, and carried him back to Penguin Island on a game-pole. The collaborators were summarily shot in the head and left for the bears. Their names had been Joe and Bob.

"You can't do this to an officer of the United States Armed Forces!" ranted General Heathcliff. His face was blue with cold and indignation, and he hung upside down from the pole like dead meat. "I've got rights under the Geneva Convention! I deserve to be treated with *respect!*"

The penguins were roughly shod in gray khakis and oversized

green fatigue army boots. Having fought with valor at the Battle of the Barracks Canteen, the Battle of the Vendomat, and the Battle of the Administrative Services Hut, they were now tired of fighting, tired of killing, and even tired of their own anger. They performed every act perfunctorily, whether it was tying their shoelaces or executing a stooge.

"Shut your goddamn yap!" barked Junior, who had distinguished himself so bravely during the recent coup d'etat that he had been placed in command of his own squadron. Junior was filled with rage for the likes of General Heathcliff, because people who took their authority for granted always reminded him of his deceased father, Whistling Pete. "You'll speak when spoken to, soldier! Or you'll end up back there on the ice with your buddies, leaking gray matter from this new ventilation duct I'm planning to drill in your forehead! How would you like that, *huh?*"

Back on Penguin Island, the natives were joyously stoking their revolutionary zeal with fancy imported liquor liberated from General Heathcliff's private reserve. Collaborators were systematically shot and buried in the snow, while prisoners were released from the barbed-wire compound and presented with high administrative positions in the provisional government.

It was a slow, generally listless procession to the outskirts of town. The General had refused a last meal, a last request, and a blindfold. He accepted a cigarette, though. A filterless menthol.

"I want to look you feather-brained bastards straight in the eyes," the General barked. It was, really, the General's finest hour, especially since his favorite movie had always been *Patton,* starring George C. Scott. "You birds don't scare me one bit, and you want to know why? Because you're silly looking, that's why. No matter how many guns you've got, or tanks, or even maybe satellite telecommunications someday, you'll still always be penguins, flapping around on frozen rocks. And I wouldn't wish that sort of humiliation on *anybody*."

"Ready!"

Junior issued the order with his arm upraised. It was important to project a sense of ceremony on such occasions. It had something to do with not letting passionate moments get too far out of hand.

"Go ahead, dream of conquest and adventure," the General told them fiercely. His hands were tied behind his back while he puffed away merrily at his cigarette. "You'll always be fat floppy birds, so far as I'm concerned. No nation on this planet will ever *respect* you."

"Aim!"

Junior watched his roughly clad troops site smartly down the barrels of their M15s, these terribly large guns that had to be braced on wooden pikes. Junior was damn proud of his boys and what they'd accomplished. For that matter, he was damn proud of himself.

"Whenever anybody looks at you they're gonna think the same thing. Look at those cute little penguins. Even if you're firing an M15 in their direction. Even if you're launching hand grenades or neutron bombs. People are gonna look at you acting tough and they're gonna say, Oh my, what a bunch of cuties; what a bunch of cute little—"

"Fire!"

It was a long moment with the sound of postponement in it. To Junior's ears, the cessation of the General's voice sounded even more loudly in the frozen air than the multiple crack of the rifles.

"I hope to teach you penguins about justice," General Heathcliff had solemnly declared on the first day of the occupation. "I hope to teach you about law. I hope to teach you about the ways of men, and the responsibilities of nations. I hope you won't look upon us as the enemy. I hope you'll think of us as friends."

Be careful what you wish for, Junior thought, regarding the General's large immobile body in the snow.

And if you're not going to be careful, then don't piss around *this* particular penguin.

At which point Junior turned his squad around and went home.

5

THE COUP

In many parts of the world, triumphant animals were proving themselves masters of the same indecencies once practiced upon them. They slaughtered human beings indiscriminately for food, or yoked them to the braces of primitive farm equipment. They wore bizarre coats and jackets sewn together from human hair and skin, and proudly displayed their barbaric couture at garden parties and political rallies. They organized gulags, rehabilitation colonies, and collective farms, and forced human prisoners to shave their heads and read aloud together from *The Collected Teachings of Mr. Big*. They even took control of local TV broadcasting centers, and began producing their own hairier versions of public programming: *The We Love Mr. Big Show*, *The We Hate Humans Show*, *The Animals Are Good Show*, and of course the wildly popular *Dave the Otter Show, Starring Mr. Big's Closest Personal Friend and Advisor, Dave the Otter*.

"I'm telling you, Dave, we gotta do something about these beggars on the streets." The caller was a Doberman from Detroit, where animals ruled over a city of flames. "It's disgusting is what it is. Them begging handouts all the time, sticking their dead babies in our faces, showing us their sores. Look, I'm willing to help out a poor human whenever I've got a few extra dollars, but most of these bums are living in nice suburban houses, driving Cadillacs and Bel Airs. They're just *disguised* as bums, don't you know? Basically, Dave, I think we've just got to make it illegal to be destitute, and punish it, you know, by like execution or something. Or maybe life service on a Collective Farm."

"Can I break in here a minute, caller?" interjected Dave the Otter, leaning earnestly across his polished desk. Dave had put on a lot of weight in the last few weeks, and his hair was slicked back with a reflective, greasy substance. "Basically I think you've brought up some good points, and we should review them at our leisure, so to speak."

With a flip of his paw, Dave the Otter cut off the Detroit caller. Then he lifted up the stack of standard review cards, which he held in his lap.

"Now the caller's first point is worth mentioning again, and"—Dave shuffled assuredly through the review cards, searching for the loaded ace—"that point is *this*."

Dave the Otter lifted the card to Camera 1 for an EXTREME CLOSE-UP. The card said:

HUMAN BEINGS ARE LIARS

"That's right, mammals and mollusks. Human beings lie, and there ain't no two ways about it. Lying is part of the genetic structure of all human-type brain systems; it has to do with the structural properties of language or something, which I can't quite go into right now, so just take my word for it, okay? And so"—taking a long, deep breath—"to return to my *first* point"—Dave the Otter held up the review card again.

HUMAN BEINGS ARE LIARS

—"and don't you forget it."

* * *

It was probably Bunny Fairchild's favorite program, since it usually concluded with the same lengthy prerecorded announcement from Mr. Big.

"I wear this hood upon my head because I do not want to be thought of as an individual," Mr. Big told his multitudes. "I wear this hood upon my head because I want to be thought of as an abstraction. You are the same animal as me. I am the same animal as you. Underneath our hoods of bone and muscle, we are all brothers and sisters. Most of us, that is, with the exception of one black bird. And that bird, as you all know, is named Charlie the Crow."

At this point an extreme frozen close-up of Charlie, clipped from another network's stock news footage, played on the screen. Charlie's mouth was open in midharangue. He was wearing sunglasses, and his face looked puffy from either too much alcohol or not enough sleep.

"Bring me this bird," Mr. Big told his multitudes, "and I will teach him how to think. He's just a mixed-up animal looking for love. And that's what we can give him, my fellow beasties. More love than he knows what to do with, and then some."

Working away industriously at the pedals of her Exercycle, immured for the second week in a row in her high-security, closed-system penthouse, Bunny enjoyed working off calories while eating Ben and Jerry's ice cream and watching TV. She had rigged the bike's calorie counter to alert her whenever she burned off enough for another spoonful of Cherry Garcia, and she liked the look of this whole new marketing possibility being presented to her by the Animal Broadcasting Network.

Using animals not to sell to humans. But using animals to sell to other animals.

Ping the bell on the Exercycle said.

And Bunny took another bite of ice cream.

"They aren't the enemy, *sir,*" Bunny informed the still-circulating memory of her old boss, who had blown his brains out two days previously with a handy Beretta from Bunny's purse. "They're an exciting new concept in customer demographics."

Like an infomercial, or a book by Norman Mailer, the Animal Broadcasting Network was frequently interrupted by advertisements for itself. In the next particular installment, random "animals on the street" were interviewed by the subjective lens of a news minicam. The question being asked today: "Do you think Mr. Big loves you, and why?"

"I think Mr. Big loves me very much," responded Roy the Gorilla slowly, as if he were working a small salmon bone around in his mouth. Roy had come to town on a large yellow bus with his fellow barnyard animals to demonstrate agrarian support for the urban revolution. "Because he says he does, that's why, and he seems like a nice guy, and I guess those are my reasons, okay? I mean, if he didn't love us, why would he work so hard to take over the world? It wouldn't make much sense, would it?"

Roy appeared slightly sunstruck by the camera, smiling too glossily into its dark lens. He was wearing a new Mets cap and a JE T'AIME, MR BIG T-shirt.

Bunny flicked off the sound with her remote control, watching the ape speak more banalities into the pale screen.

This isn't the enemy, Bunny thought. This isn't some wild beast on a tear. This is just a normal, average guy who works hard all day making money to spend. He enjoys buying things, and consuming brightly wrapped perishables. He wants to be the same as everybody else. And what's more—he actually *likes* being on TV.

Watching Roy the Gorilla was like a revelation to Bunny, an indication of presence.

"Christ," Bunny thought out loud. "I *love* marketing!"

Causing the bright little bell on her Exercycle to measure this moment of serendipity with a *ping.*

The President awoke from a thin drowse, dreaming of a white wooly bear performing on the high wire with a pink lacy parasol. When he was a child, the President had loved to watch trained animals at the circus. Unfortunately, though, he wasn't a child any longer. Now he was all grown up.

After the screening the President was rushed out to his limousine by security people. Fleets of motorcycled police officers greeted him with engines revving. Sharpshooters on rooftops. Gleaming sheets of bulletproof glass.

"We've got the latest reports out of Washington, Mr. President—"

"Mr. Big just broadcast his list of demands—"

"The Kremlin's on the line, Mr. President, and we think they've been drinking—"

"Your wife's been subpoenaed by Congress for being too smart—"

The President didn't know what he liked most, the information or the attention. He sat in back of the limousine while faces peered in at him through the windows. They were eavesdropping over the limousine's intercom system. They were awaiting his next move at switchboard desks all over the world.

It's time to do something, Mr. President, everybody was telling him. It's time for you to take the first step.

"Well, it's decided," the President snapped. He wasn't going down in any history books as some Nervous Nellie. He was the goddamn President of the United States, for Christ's sake.

"What's that, Mr. President?"

Someone would have to tell the First Lady he wouldn't be home for tea.

"The nearest highway and step on it," the President told his driver. "We're taking this motorcade straight to New York."

PART 9

THE END

1

CAMPUS NOVEL

Having given up on the so-called real world, Buster and Charlie had taken refuge in a Midwestern Cultural Studies Department. Being just about the only authentic animal lecturer on the market that year, Charlie had been offered a generous "recruitment package," which featured an associate-level salary, faculty housing, health benefits, a meal card, and even a researcher's supplement for Buster. In exchange Charlie agreed to deliver two lectures per week in Animal Ideology for the department's new Colonial Studies Program, as well as make regular appearances at all faculty benefits and public luncheons.

"Learn to read books for yourselves," Charlie tried to tell his students every Tuesday and Thursday afternoon at one. Noisily digesting their beef-burger lunches, Charlie's students slumped heavily against their desks, propping open their eyes with pencils and fingernails. Many were entering the REM stage of sleep even before Charlie had opened his briefcase on the podium. "You're gonna spend your life being told *how* to read, which is a lot worse than being told *what* to read, believe you me, and I guess that's about the only knowledge I've got to impart to you guys this afternoon. What time is it now—one-oh-five? Well, I guess that leaves us another hour and a half to kill. Do you guys have any questions, or would you prefer to go home for a nice little nap?"

Lapses like these left Charlie's students feeling slightly befuddled and obscure. For once in their young lives an authority figure was asking them if they wanted to do something they actually *wanted* to do. They were certain it was a trick question.

"Are you saying, Professor," ventured an Honors Student in the back row, "that all systems of social or political discourse betray some Heideggerian presumption-towards-being?"

"Sure," Charlie said, waving at the question as if it were somebody's secondhand smoke. "If you think that's what I mean, then that's good enough for me."

"Or are you saying," ventured a graduate student in the front row, who was auditing Charlie's class in order to prepare herself for an impending M.A. oral, "that socially defined gender roles limit the polyphasic potentiality of feminine discourse?"

"You've taken the words right out of my mouth," Charlie replied, smiling and happy for one of the few times in his life.

"And if I get this straight," ventured a young, retro-attired woman in the middle row, wearing a tie-dyed T-shirt and a long flowery skirt, "you're saying, like, we could just get up and *leave?* I mean, just go back to our dorms and take a *nap,* or whatever we *wanted?*" She was hugging her dense, unlovely Sociology textbooks as if they might protect her.

The entire class roused into one long murmurous accord, like an ocean awakening to itself. This didn't happen too often in a university classroom—this immediate consensual *interest.*

"Like I said, take a nap, read a book, watch TV, whatever." Charlie loved to see the dawning of knowledge in all those luminous young eyes. "I mean, this whole education thing is pretty much up to you guys, okay? And if you're *not* interested in education, well. That's okay, too."

Like universities in the Middle Ages, higher education these days had turned into a state of siege. Ever since the outbreak of civil strife, tanks, gun emplacements, and barbed-wire barricades had been erected around the college perimeter, both to protect the students from the outlying community and the outlying community from the students. This was because the world outside the school was filled with insurrections, mutiny, discord, and bad faith. And because the world inside the school was filled with students who liked to get pissed out of their minds and run over mailboxes in their cars.

Every day while Charlie lectured, attended committee meetings, and held office hours, Buster amused himself no end with the pastoral perks of college life. He woke late, breakfasted on tea and croissants at a nearby dorm, walked on the grassy knolls, lazed in the sun, and watched attractive young students flick dull plastic Frisbees across the blue sky. There were butterflies this spring, blossoming cherry trees, lemonade stands, girls in halter-tops, and bright birds visiting from all over the continent. Orioles, bluejays, starlings, and variously pheronomed finches. But no matter where they hailed from, they all sang the same sad song, and more sweetly than Buster ever imagined possible before.

They're coming to get Buster and Charlie
Tra-la-la, la-la-la, la-la-laaah.
They're coming to get Buster and Charlie
Tra-la-la, la-la-la, la-la-laaah.

These days the story of Buster and Charlie's impending assassination featured prominently on evening news programs, the front pages of national tabloids, and the wide spreading animal grapevine, but Buster didn't care anymore. There was no use crying over spilt milk—life with Whistling Pete had taught him that. And there were some things you simply couldn't change—life with Charlie had taught him that.

"Hey, like, wow, you're that penguin, aren't you?"

Occasionally Buster was approached by gangly, celebrity-struck students. They folded long skeins of hair out of their eyes and offered Buster generous helpings of beer, cigarettes, and marijuana.

"I'm sorry?" Buster replied modestly. "Can I help you with something?"

"You *are*, aren't you? And you travel around with that black bird, what's his name, he's on TV all the time. Charlie, that's right. Charlie the Crow."

Buster looked off across the ivy-entangled buildings, the defunct water fountains and underfrequented bookstores. He didn't see any remote ivory towers anywhere, but that didn't mean he would ever stop looking.

"And like you're in a whole pile of trouble or something, right? The animals hate you, and the humans hate you, and you're like totally unpopular, like Madonna or somebody. Oh wow. I can't believe this. Hey, everybody! Look here! I just met Buster the Penguin!"

2

FIFTEEN MINUTES

Capt. Jack Hollister and Sgt. Yuri Rudityev were doing forty-three miles an hour on the interstate through Pennsylvania, the Plains States, and South Dakota, making love all the way like hormone-struck adolescents. Their ride was an Abrams M1 Main Battle Tank, which, much like Hollister himself, was slow on the straightaways, but could take any curve with the best of them. It was equipped with a 105mm. M68A1 cannon, one .50 and two 7.62mm. MGs, air safety bags, and power brakes. The steering console was on automatic pilot. Jackson Browne was playing softly on the dashboard stereo.

"You're a really special individual, Yuri," Captain Hollister whispered under his breath, zipping up his green fatigue army pants and buckling his gray cloth belt. He was sucking on a breath mint and feeling the deep diesel hum of the Lycoming AGT-1500 gas turbine in his bones. "And I mean that sincerely, Yuri. Not only are you unafraid of compassion—you're unafraid to be a man. And that's a really unusual combination to discover in any guy these days, especially a Russian-born lifer like yourself. You're too good for women, Yuri. You deserve a love more permanent and enduring than all that messy, yucky bumping in the night, all those expensive meals and overpriced greeting cards. In fact, now that I think about it, Yuri, you're probably too good for *me.*"

It was impossible to tell how much Yuri understood of what was happening between him and his commanding officer. Immured within his carapace of bandages, all Yuri did anymore was squirm continuously and utter the same muffled epithets.

Though their mission lacked all the official sanctions of a military maneuver, it still qualified as what was known in NSC circles as an "unconfirmed covert op." Just in the last few days or so, somebody's commanding officer had let it be known to somebody *else's* commanding officer that if a couple of unnamed former intelligence types were to, you know, "borrow" a particular piece of military hardware for the weekend, and that, say, this aforementioned military equipment were to be involved in the subsequent annihilation of two avian-revolutionary types practicing PC anti-Americanism at some bohunk land-grant liberal arts university, well. Let's just say there'd be no questions asked. And if those former intelligence types were to vanish into the woodwork immediately afterward? Well, it was no skin off the *Company's* nose, was it?

"We're projecting a target approach of fourteen hundred hours Midwestern time, Yuri." Now that Hollister was back in the driver's seat he was all business, snapping toggles, punching digital displays, and adjusting the dashboard stereo's balance and tone controls. On the cassette deck Jackson Browne was letting everybody know that, having endured the love of a bad woman, he was still *alive.*

Hollister couldn't have sung the lyrics any better himself.

"Those damn birds have hid out in the one place they thought we'd never find them," Hollister declared. "A place with books in it, Yuri. A dream world completely cut off from reality and populated by nothing but long-haired hippie girls who'll roll in the hay with practically *anybody.* Big Negro quarterbacks and pituitary-freak basketball players, stealing educational opportunities from strong, equally deprived *white* boys like ourselves. Female sportscasters, Asian chemistry teachers, fluoridated water. An entire town filled with young people who want to do nothing but lie in the sun all day, drink beer, and have sexual relations with their professors. It makes my heart sick, Yuri. It makes me want to cough up my own bile. In a world falling apart even as we speak, all these Gen-X *kids* want to do is masturbate while watching rock videos on MTV."

Hollister couldn't stop clenching and unclenching the .50mm. firing trigger as they climbed over the smooth amber hills into Wyoming.

This was the real world, Hollister thought to himself. This rolling piece of thunderous malevolent metal.

Then, out of the thrumming darkness, Captain Hollister heard them coming. Skimming across the surface of the spinning Animal Planet like angels propelled by wings of song.

The dashboard radar screen lit up with a blizzard of blips.

"I think we've got company," Hollister sang softly, lighting up a Cigarillo.

At which point the fleet of news-watch helicopters came swooping down for a live-on-the-scene exclusive.

All across the university, public and private televisions alike were tuned to the same news channel.

"Is this war, Captain?"

"No. It's a surgical strike."

"Has the World Court approved your actions?"

"Screw the World Court. Don't you support our boys in uniform?"

"Have Charlie and his penguin friend really done anything so serious that they *deserve* being blown away with a howitzer?"

"Are you calling me un-American? Are you questioning my integrity as a military representative of this mighty nation? I've fought animal anarchists all my life, lady—not like you liberal media queens with your wine and cheese soirees. Not like those earring-wearing, twenty-something bureaucrats in Congress! I've been decorated more than a dozen times, and so has my . . . well, my friend Yuri, here. We're cops of the world and you can't blame us for doing our job, can you? It's an ugly job and someone's got to do it."

Charlie and Buster had come out to a high, grassy knoll on

the edge of campus. They could hear televised voices resounding in the air like a ghost of history.

"Oh well," Buster said. "I never finished my memoirs, Charlie, and now I never will. I'll never fly in a hot-air balloon. I'll never sleep with a virgin. I'll never get that cosmetic surgery, you know, to get rid of this double chin I'm so self-conscious about? I'll never visit California, I'll never learn to speak French, I'll never have kids, and I'll never see my wife, Sandy, again. But that's okay, Charlie. In order to see the world, you have to pay a price. And considering how far I've been and how much I've seen, I consider the cost to have been worth it."

They could hear the escorting fleet of journalists heading their way before they could see the actual military hardware. The journalists were riding in big, overcrowded yellow buses, drinking beers and watching sporting events on battery-operated televisions. Boom mikes extended weirdly from racing jeeps and minivans like robotic appendages. The Abrams tank was puny in comparison to all the hoopla surrounding it. Bathed by a bank of 100,000-watt mobile klieg lights, it looked flat and dull colored, like a tatty carpet on wheels.

Charlie was ready. Even more ready than Buster.

"Looks like we've got company," Charlie said.

Then he sat down beside Buster on the green grass and waited for something to happen.

At the same time Hollister, Yuri, and the news media were approaching from the west, Rick the Husky was taking a rocky shortcut up a disused fire road and approaching even more rapidly from the southeast.

"Muk Luk *tired*. Muk Luk don't want to get up. Muk Luk want to *sleep*."

Muk Luk was curled up in the backseat with her whiskey.

Wanda was shaking her by the shoulders and splashing tepid water on her face from a bottle of Evian.

"You've *got* to get up, Muk Luk. You've got to do what you do best. Or there won't *be* any Buster around to feel mournful about. Just think of it, Muk Luk. How terribly you'd miss him *then.*"

Underneath her mound of parkas, Muk Luk had come unhinged from all her clothing except the long underwear. Her skin was denuded of hair and muscle tone from weeks of self-neglect, making her look as spindly as an unshelled sea tortoise. Her limbs rolled loosely when Wanda shook them.

On the dashboard radio, the President's motorcade was being covered live on CSPAN-FM: "Tell the penguins we *want* to negotiate!" the President's voice barked at his crowd of advisors,

> and that this *isn't* an ultimatum. And while we're all, how do I put this, quote, deeply saddened by the loss of one of our nation's finest military commanders, unquote, we remain willing to provide long-term international economic incentives and U.N. Charter resolutions to protect the sovereignty of their silly little island—oh, dammit, Max. Promise them anything—just make it clear we want to send weapons inspectors into the Penguin Island Nuclear Reactor and shut the damn thing *off*—

Rick clicked off the radio and took the summit in third gear. The old Pontiac rocked wildly, diving through heavy brambles and extinguished campfires. The engine cut out for a moment—Rick jumped the clutch—and sparks reignited again as momentum took hold.

Suddenly the entire campus appeared in full view below them like an outdoor stage set, all even green lawns and tidy brick buildings.

"Come on, Muk Luk!" Rick shouted. "Stop feeling sorry for yourself and get it together! You're a goddamn Eskimo and they're no match for you! So pull up your knickers and let's get cooking! We're running out of time, Muk Luk! And so are Charlie and Buster!"

3

MEDIA EVENT

First-run commercial revenue alone was predicted in the high jillions, and the event was already being broadcast live on three-hundred-plus cable and world-network channels simultaneously. This was the sort of all-out mainstream product approval rating that marketing people once dreamed about as a theoretical absolute. Total Entertainment Value. Everybody had studied the idea back in business school, but nobody had believed it actually possible before.

"It's bigger than Foreman vs. Ali!" exclaimed the various development directors of Worldco Books, Worldco Films, and Worldco Home Entertainment, venturing hesitantly outside the lead-shielded doors of their corporate bomb shelters and blinking at the noon sun. "It's bigger than Woodstock Four! It's bigger than Bobby Riggs and Billie Jean King! It's bigger than martians landing from outer space! It's bigger than the goddamn end of the world!"

A stillness had descended even over the riot-dazed streets of America's cities, where a few random animals continued wandering listlessly about.

"So what do you think, Charlie?" The announcer was shoving his microphone into Charlie's face like a statement of fact. "Now that you're pretty much finished, have you got any last words for everybody at home?"

"Not really," Charlie replied, chewing laconically on a long dandelion stem. "I figure that everybody watching at home's a grown adult, regardless of species or gender. Let them figure it out for themselves."

"Are you saying you've renounced political action, Charlie?"

"I haven't renounced it. I'm just not wasting it on you guys."

"Isn't that a little unfair, Charlie? After all, we here at the media don't invent the news. We just report it."

"Yeah," Charlie said. "Yeah, *sure.*"

All over the Animal Planet, the slumbering beast was starting to rouse.

"Hello, Bunny? This is Jack, Bart's replacement over at Worldco Books and Entertainment—"

"—Hello. This is Bunny Fairchild, and I'm either in a meeting, or else conducting a high six-figure paperback auction right now—"

"Bunny? Hey, I said it's Jack from Product Development. Are you screening this call?"

"—But if you'll leave your name and number at the sound of the beep—"

"I *left* my goddamn name and number twenty minutes ago. Are you avoiding me, Bunny? Our Publisher warned me about this. He *said* you might try avoiding me—"

"—and I'll get right back to you. And by the way, if you're calling about the new Sandy the Penguin Advertising promotion I've been discussing with Sears and the May Co. recently, I'm afraid, as they say, that the deal's already done. Better luck next time. And bye."

Jack slammed down the phone and spun around in his leather upholstered swivel chair. Jack's immediate predecessor, Bart, had been slow to respond to a crisis, and look what happened to *him.*

Jack couldn't help gazing around philosophically at Bart's old office, which had been reduced by the recent "incident" to a pocket catastrophe. Splintered furniture was strewn haphazardly among broken-spined Sales Reports, torn hardback best-sellers, and petrified punctuations of animal dung.

Jack picked up the phone and punched another number.

"Hello? Who the fuck is this?"

"Hello, Stan. This is Jack, Bart's replacement over at Worldco."

"Oh yeah? Well fuck you, Jack! And fuck all you bastards over at Worldco!"

"Look, Stan, no hard feelings, okay?"

"Fuck your no-hard-feelings, Jack! You know where I am right now? I'm hiding under the bed with my fucking wife and I haven't bathed or eaten in three days! My apartment looks like fucking Berlin, *Jack*. And I blame it all on you bastards at Worldco!"

"You're a businessman, Stan."

"And you're an asshole, Jack!"

"And we're not enemies, Stan. We both believe in the same things, don't we? The right to bear firearms, the all-knowing supremacy of a God who loves us, and the free-enterprise system."

"I believe you're a fucking shithead, Jack. And so's that fucking cunt of yours, Bunny Fairchild."

"I only want to say six words to you, Stan."

"My cleaning lady left me for those Animal Anarchists, and I haven't been laid in three weeks!"

"And those six words are these."

Jack spoke evenly, one word at a time. He kept reminding himself that Stan Garfield was a consummate professional who knew a good business proposition when he heard one.

"Yeah?" Stan ventured slowly.

It wasn't a response. Like a zero in the sales figures, it acted more like a place holder.

"We," Jack said.

"Okay so far."

"Want."

"I'm listening, shit brain."

"To."

"Come to Papa, Jack."

"Make."

"I'm still listening."

"A."

"And this better be good."

"Deal."

Another long, significant pause. A place holder big enough to pay both their salaries forever.

"You want to make a deal, huh?"

"That's right, Stan."

Static hissed on the line. Somewhere out there in cyberspace, the entire world was listening.

"Oh yeah?" Stan replied. "Then you boys better stop pissing me around."

Faxes, cellular phones, E-mail, express couriers, and conference calls were all soon getting in on the act, making the entire Animal Planet hum with heat and information. Things and ideas began to make themselves known. Identities emerged from the corporate rubble. Brand names and copyright insignia clambered out of ruined cities and subway systems. Somewhere deep within the near-dormant ember of the world-business network, an entire system of meaning was beginning to speak again. And the only word it wanted to speak anymore was *itself*.

"—I don't care if you *tried* to reach Bunny Fairchild—I'm saying *try again!* And who's that homosexual over at Twentieth Century Fox? Get *him* on the line too—"

"—I want a conversion clause in this contract to match the conversion clause I *should've* gotten in the *last* contract—"

"—I've got Stan Garfield on line one, sir—"

"—Oh yeah? Well *fuck* Stan Garfield!"

"—Oh yeah? Well fuck you too, you cheap motherfucker—"

"—We've got an audience rating of ninety-nine point eight percent, and that's only because the other point-two percent are dying, asleep, or going to the bathroom—"

"—Slow down the cocksuckers in the armored vehicle—close up on the Eskimo chick—and I wanta see more cleavage on the ape babe, and I mean *pronto*—"

"—I want a line of doll merchandise on the shelves by this afternoon and I don't care if the stores *have* just been looted, we're talking about your *job* lady—"

"—I'm saying it again, I want to speak with Bunny eff, ay, eye, are, sea, aitch, eye, ell, dee—"

"—Jack O'Malley on five, Mr. Garfield—"

"—Hello, Stan? There's a glitch in production and we won't have our merchandise in the stores until tomorrow morning—"

"—Oh *yeah?*—"

"—But we're still trying to reach Bunny over at CMA—they say she's out of town on *business,* Stan. What's that bitch up to, anyway—"

"Well, *fuck* your glitch in production, Jack! Did you hear me! Just fuck fuck fuck fuck *you!*"

It wasn't even their denouement anymore. Their lives belonged to somebody else now.

Sprawled on the green grass, Buster and Charlie watched the

world of culture mobilize itself around them like an army of misinformation. Humans were aiming video cameras and boom mikes at them from every horizon. They didn't want to miss a move either Charlie or Buster made, yet they didn't seem to care a whit what might about to them.

"Human beings have manufactured a lot of really amazing things in this world," Charlie conceded, chewing his soggy dandelion and enjoying the warm sun on his back. "But the one thing they sure do a lousy job with is space. Just look, Buster. They pour concrete over everything. They park a million smog-belching cars in every available lot. They plant down these hard, really uncomfortable bus benches that nobody but a homeless person would *ever* want to sit on, and then what do they do? They chase those homeless people off, as if there's a queue of *reputable* people right behind them just *dying* to make hemorrhoids for themselves. Human beings should be left to do what they do best: manufacturing cookies, soda water, really bad Sylvester Stallone movies, and Levi's. But when it comes to space, man, leave it to old Mother Nature. I know there's the goddamn bugs and everything, but at least the green grass has a little texture to it. At least I can lie out on the soft ground without blistering my sore butt."

Buster had never seen so many people spending so much money in order to understand so little. Within just the past few hours, human beings had flooded the campus with portable gift shops and fast-food restaurants. They had begun selling commemorative T-shirts and puzzling plastic doodads out of burlap tents and the backs of old pickup trucks. It was impossible to doubt the incredible industry of human beings, Buster thought. But what the hell they were on about—that was a different story.

"We're not even animals to them, are we, Charlie?" Buster was watching multiplied images of himself being played on ballpark-sized video monitors mounted over the main road. "We're not even flesh and blood. It's like they've sucked all the meaning out of us, isn't it, Charlie? They've sucked out every inch of animal flesh until all they've got left to show for us is our skin and our beaks."

Charlie thought about this for a moment. Then he reached over and gave his friend's wing a firm squeeze.

"Human beings are a trip, aren't they, old pal? I mean, how could a bunch of hairless bipeds be so smart and act so stupid?"

It was the first time Charlie, in all their many months together, had ever ventured to touch him. Buster liked this moment. He wanted it to last.

"That's a good question, Charlie," Buster replied.

But it wasn't a question anybody in the world seemed poised to answer.

Rick the Husky didn't like the look of things one bit.

"We seem to be driving in the only direction we're allowed to go," he told his friends. "And I don't know about you guys. But that idea makes me *really* nervous."

Outside their car, the fleets of news vans and crowd-control emergency vehicles had shut down all roads leading on or off campus. Everywhere Rick drove, he was directed down crowded thoroughfares by men and women wielding orange Day-Glo batons.

"Make way for the Eskimo!" shouted highway patrolmen through their high-tech car megaphones. "Make way for the Eskimo!"

Wanda was entranced by all the lights and glamor of it.

"You know, this could be my big break," she told herself, plucking her eyebrows in her flicking gold compact. "I mean, bigger careers have amounted from less."

"Grrr," Rick muttered deep in his throat. The hair on the back of his neck began to bristle.

196

As they were ushered through a gauntlet of cameras and audio-processing equipment, a crowd of jogging news reporters swept around their car like a blizzard of locusts, gobbling up every bit of stray grain in sight.

"Has Muk Luk kept up with her training?"

"Could this be regarded as a sort of 'grudge-match'?"

"Where do you fit into all this, Rick? Were you ever abused as a pup? Have you ever been abducted by a UFO?"

"Wanda, Wanda, can we have a word with you, Wanda?"

"Yes!" Wanda shouted. She was trying to roll down her window. She was trying to unlatch her door. "I'll answer any question! I'll help you as much as I can!"

But Rick was in control of the dashboard electrical panel. He rolled up all the windows with a squeaky whine of rubber and glass. Then he activated all the interior locks with a solid, unified click.

"Rick! Stop! Open the windows! Please let me talk!"

Rick regarded Wanda's look of amazement in the rearview mirror. She wasn't herself anymore. She was just that awful animal presence the cameras wanted her to be.

"Grrr," Rick told her. "Stop embarrassing yourself. We've got a job to do."

Released from Wanda's frantic arms, Muk Luk moaned and slid to the floor with a thump.

"No point in nothing," she muttered. "No place worth going, no way, no how. Muk Luk just want to go home to her igloo-tract housing and never come back. Living so close to the equator makes human beings totally nuts."

The Culture Industry was generating its own momentum now, and doing what it did best. Processing time and selling it off in bright tiny packages. Reinventing the same old ideas that had been invented a zillion times before. Duplicating and reduplicating every image that had ever been manufactured and storing them all on CD, microchip, and laser disc.

"The tank's on the green—"

"We've got closeups of the crowd—"

"We've got closeups of the tank—"

"We've got closeups of Charlie and the penguin—hey, could somebody make them look alive out there! They're sitting on their butts getting a bloody *suntan*— "

"We've got a closeup of the ape lady's cleavage, of Rick at the wheel smoking a charred cigarette butt, of Muk Luk swooning loosely in Wanda's voluptuous arms—"

"What a barker—"

"What knobs—"

"Who's that on line two?"

"Who the fuck you *think* it is on line two, you fucking four-eyed collegiate piece of mandrill shit! I want action! I want passion! I want lesbo-love between the ape lady and the Eskimo! I want—I want—I want—ugh—ugh—ugh—ugh—"

"Is that interference?"

"I think it's a mild coronary—"

"—ugh—ugh—I want—I want—that's better, just a glass of water and get Bunny Fairchild on the line *rightthisgoddamn-minute*—I want a big fucking finale! You hear me! I want that tank to blast them into fucking smithereens! I want planes exploding! I want buildings collapsing! I want you to shove fire-works up everybody's asshole and blast them to the fucking *moon*— "

"Camera five on Car two. Camera four on Car one. We've got surface movement on the artillery. We've got a reaction shot from the penguin. But somebody, somebody somewhere, could *somebody* make those guys look *alive* out there!"

"And *cut* to the President on Six—"

"—despite the terrible inequalities existing between animals and humans, that ours is a nation of compromise, and not of division. A people of magnitude, and not of bias. A culture of reconciliation, and not of—that's right, and so on and so forth, recycle some old LBJ speeches or something. And as for our meeting with Mister Big, just say we got on well, and that I described him as a, quote, noble, God-fearing, practically a Baptist-type of individual, unquote. But mainly that the resumption of normal Manhattan business hours is being discussed as a quote real possibility unquote and on all other inquiries stamp a no comment on that, okay? Over."

"And *cut* to Copter two. We've got the tank on the green. We've got the tank rolling over student blankets and Styrofoam beer containers. We've got a live eyewitness account on Camera four. And *cut* to Four."

"Things have gotten pretty hairy in the last few minutes of the competition, wouldn't you say, sir? And I hope you're not offended by the term 'hairy.' "

"Not at all, Mr. Newscaster, I have taken no offense whatsoever. Is that camera live? Am I actually on TV?"

"You sure are, sir, and do you mind if I ask? What's your name and where are you from?"

"My name is Roy the Gorilla and I hale from, well, Africa originally, but these days I live on a pretty big corporate farm down in a friendly state I like to call Georgia."

"Up for the holidays, are you?"

"I'm here with the Mr. Big bus tour, which has been a very educational experience, and has introduced me to many lovely females of many different species and nationalities—"

"And your thoughts on the current action out there on the field?"

"Well, I like Charlie okay, and I think the penguin is really cute. But I like the army a lot, too, and I know they must work really hard at their jobs. So I guess I kind of hope Charlie does-n't get killed. But at the same time, I want the army people to be successful, too, since they're probably very hardworking and all—"

"And *cut* to the tank on the green—"

"And *cut* to Charlie and Buster—"

"And *cut* to the Eskimo babe—"

"Now, Muk Luk! *Now!*"

They had propped her against the hood of the Rambler, the spear cocked in her throwing hand like the Liberty Torch. They were being filmed from every conceivable angle by media rep-resentatives of the world's most-favored-nations trading partners.

It was so weird, Rick thought. Like my life's already a rerun even before it's happened.

At which point Muk Luk's eyes rolled back into her feverish head and she swooned, sliding down the surface of the car and collapsing on the green, overilluminated grass.

Wanda picked up Muk Luk's battered spear and showed it to Rick with a weird look of dissociation, as if it were a size 20 ball gown, when everybody in the world knew Wanda was a size 18.

"Jesus, Rick. What are we supposed to do with *this?*"

The media were impartial. This meant that nobody who worked for them ever got in the way of increasing their own revenue.

"Cut to the tank—"

"Cut to the weapon arm being raised—"

"Cut to Charlie—"

"Cut to the penguin—"

"Cut to the blue sky—"

"Cut to the green grass—"

All over the world, humans and animals alike were tuned to the same already-scheduled event-about-to-happen.

"Well, old buddy, I guess this is it."

"I guess so, Charlie. It just seems to be taking so *long*."

Charlie gave Buster that same cynical look one more time.

"You just don't get it, do you, buddy?"

"What's that, Charlie?"

"They're making room for more *commercials*."

And then the tank was on the green. And Charlie and Buster were gazing dully into the eye of the humming weapon. And the sky was filled with helicopters.

And then it happened.

    It happened.

        And then it happened.

After billions spent on cameras, guns, road food, cheap dates, minority sports casters, digital sound, CD-ROM, simulcast stereo, local research, location coordinators, communication degrees, film school, corporate lawsuits, and bad love. The one thing everybody feared and nobody could prevent.

Nothing.

Nothing happened.

"Someone cue the tank—"

"We've cued the tank—"

"What are those bozos doing in there?"

"Someone open the hatch. We're taking down the cameras. We've got the hatch door open. We're into the tank. We see human movement. We see two men rolling around on the floor, oh Christ— Cut—Cut—Cut, I said—*Cut!*—For chrissakes, *CUT!*"

The moment of fulfillment had been too much for Jack Hollister and his adjutant, Yuri Rudityev, to bear.

When the cameras found them they were rolling around on the floor of the Abrams, making love like there was no tomorrow.

4

THE BIG FINALE

"Most of those animals down there aren't any different from you or me," Bunny Fairchild told her guest in the helicopter's rear cabin, gazing out at the media-wrought multitudes, the hastily erected shopping kiosks, the steaming barbecue grills, and the trailer-bound recreational boats. "They want too much from life, and all they're ever given is too little. They wake up, go to school, get a job, have babies, take a series of terrible holidays, suffer pointlessly, and, just as pointlessly, die. They attend school holiday productions, yard sales, political rallies, sporting events, RV and boat shows. They may not know what they want, but they do know they want something beautiful. They look and look, but when they get tired of looking, they come to us. And we try to help."

Down below, the Presidential motorcade had drawn a bold dark arrow straight to the heart of the assembled news cameras and technical support crews. The President was already delivering one of his most heartfelt orations from the summit of a firm wooden podium. The human and animal onlookers listened distractedly, waiting for something important to happen.

"We offer them all the truth and justice we've given up finding for ourselves," Bunny said softly. As the helicopter began to bank, swoop, and descend, she felt a lightness in her chest, a sense of freedom and possibility. "I'm not saying we're better than anybody else, exactly. But we give those poor dumb animals something to believe in besides themselves. And that's all they're looking for, you know. Something besides themselves."

The President was saying over the loudspeakers, "Let us not divide ourselves into warring factions, but work together, nobly and gloriously, in manufacturing new products, and promoting them proudly in the international shopping mall of our new global economy—"

The crowds, though, were waiting for something else, and when the helicopter came down onto the tarmac, their expectations began to rouse. They had come here to see justice, but all they found was another high-ranking government official, and another fleet of eyewitness-news minicams.

But now, finally, that someone else was coming. Someone they hadn't been expecting until now.

"It's time," Bunny told her guest as they set down on the field with a little bump. The rotors stirred up candy wrappers and discarded program booklets like secondhand confetti. "We won't keep them waiting any longer. We're already here."

Then she escorted Mr. Big out across the windy tarmac to address the President and his multitudes.

PART 10

AND AFTER

1

PUBLIC SERVICE

Charlie and Buster were convicted of treason, flight from prosecution, extortion of public confidence, and displaying prematurely anti-authoritarian sentiments without the benefit of acceptable profit motivation. Sentenced to death by a court triumvirate of their peers, they were remanded to the custody of the new Animal Containment Division of the Criminal Court System, where their sentence was eventually commuted to life imprisonment after a last-minute mercy plea by their court-appointed legal representative, Dave the Otter.

"Let's face it, guys," Dave told the legal boys upstairs. "You don't like 'em, I don't like 'em, but how would it look, frying some cute little penguin on public TV? The way I figure, this is supposed to be a new, more compassionate sort of government, right? So I say we lock the jokers in a big hole in the ground and throw away the key. Fry 'em and we make 'em look bigger than life. But bury 'em in a hole, and we make 'em look punier than metal."

The years passed quietly and uneventfully in a small wire mesh cell about the size of a refrigerator-freezer. The cell included a porcelain loo, a water dispenser, a transistor radio, and a bunkbed. While time passed them by, they read books and magazines, played round-robin checkers championships with other prisoners on the block, and were hosed down every few days or so by their cordial and well-meaning security guard.

"When Nietzsche made such a big deal out of the eternal recurrence, I wonder if he was talking about popular culture," Charlie wondered out loud. He was gripping the wire-mesh walls while cold water was fired at him from a long green garden hose. "It used to be that fads came and went. Now they just stay and stay. Do you know kids today are still listening to the Rolling Stones and the Beach Boys, and those phoney old dudes are like in their *fifties?* Rap music's still here. Even radio drama. The Ku Klux Klan'll never leave. Neither will the Democrats, the Republicans, the Hollywood movie industry, *I Love Lucy,* Frisbees, Play-Doh, The Flat-Earth Society, the Coneheads, James Bond, Mighty Mouse, or the Evil Empire. By insisting on being always new, popular culture constantly ends up being nothing but eternally the same. Freedom is no longer a state of being, man. It's now a high marketing concept."

Outside their still-dripping cage, Roy the Gorilla rewound the green garden hose onto the iron spigot and smiled.

"I sure enjoy listening to you say such interesting things, Charlie," Roy said. "Being your guys' trustee here at the animal prison has turned out to be a really great job, don't you think?"

Their only visitor was Rick the Husky, who arrived every few weeks or so bearing the latest news from home, and a picnic basket packed with Spam sandwiches and coleslaw.

"Wanda's in Frisco," he told them as he doled out postprandial smokes, "selling lingerie at this new boutique she opened downtown. Ladies' lingerie, mostly, but she still manages to sell an occasional animal garment out of the back room. Wanda's got a Social Security card and a tax accountant, and to hear her go on about it, you'd think she's now Crown Princess of Arabia or something. Oh, hadn't you heard? Now that animals are accepted members of the new global economy, they're allowed to pay taxes. Pity about health care, though."

On days when Rick visited, Buster and Charlie would pull up close to the mesh and exchange the latest letters from their friends on the outside. Surprisingly enough, most of the news they received was either downright good, or nowhere near as bad as they expected.

Dear Black Bird and Buster,
   Weather stinks. What's new.
   Muk Luk over her dejection. Muk Luk also dating some very curious-looking corporate types who have taken over Dave's Trading Post. Muk Luk stop trying to make strange, pale gentlemen drunk and seduce them with hand jobs, though. Now she just hammer them over the head with axe handle and drag them home on her sled.
   Sometimes Muk Luk feel violence is not the answer. Other times she think maybe these guys deserve it.
   Muk Luk think of you both often and hope you write soon.

                    Love always,
                    Muk Luk the Eskimo

"I don't care what I or others may have said in the past about her looks," Charlie concluded after reading one of Muk Luk's crayon-scrawled missives. "But that Eskimo chick sure has *class.*"

Buster tried to write back, but he never managed more than a few shallow, contrived phrases. *Very good to hear from you.* Or *When I think of all the mistakes I've made.* He knew there was something he still had to tell Muk Luk. He just didn't happen to know what it was.

Outside in the supposedly real world, animals and men had organized themselves into a whole new scheme of cultural demographics. For the first time in the recorded history of western civilization, animals were being hired as sales representatives, production managers, and even executive board members of companies that produced children's toys, rock and roll music, and liquified petroleum gas. They were permitted to send their children to public schools, shop at local supermarkets, and vote for their own state and federal congressional leaders. Cities were redistricted in order to create new animal-enterprise zones (though admittedly not in the best parts of town) and, not too long after that, even the entertainment industry began to boast full integration of both its work staff and celebrity personnel. After centuries of mindless, foolish, and often economically unfeasible divisiveness, the world was finally coming together. Humans and animals alike just had to *believe.*

"Our day has finally arrived," Mister Big announced nightly on his nationally syndicated late-night TV talk show, which was currently sponsored by Purina Dog Chow and the Florida Orange Growers Association. "United we shall prevail, work hard, achieve financial progress, and eventually acquire our own glamorous automobiles. Now please, go out there and live your lives to the fullest. And while you're at it, please purchase many helpings of dog chow and orange juice, because I want you to take good care of yourselves. Never doubt for a moment, my fellow beasties, Mr. Big loves you all!"

Of course there were more prisons, but nobody talked too much about *them*. For example, the new federally funded Animal Containment Division in which Buster and Charlie were currently incarcerated boasted one of the largest prison populations in the free world, nearly fourteen thousand inmates filed away in a beehive of tiny, smelly cells that often lacked proper toilets and sanitary facilities. For the most part, Charlie and Buster's cell mates were mammals who had been convicted of violent, "victim-intensive" crimes. Armed robberies and car jackings, burglaries and sexual assaults. According to opinion polls, criminal types like Buster and Charlie were selfish, sociopathic personalities who refused to respond to rehabilitation programs—not that there were that many to choose from.

"We either work in the prison laundry," Buster explained to Rick during one of his visits, "or attend group therapy sessions in the psychiatric ward. I started making this belt out of beads, you know? But then, after a while, I guess I kind of lost interest."

Rick, who was going slightly gray at the temples, had long ago run out of consolatory advice for his friends. He no longer discussed things like signature drives, or parole hearings, or even Presidential pardons—all of which had proved consistently unrewarding efforts in the past. Usually he just dropped off whatever newspapers and chocolates he had picked up at the Prison Gift Shop, then curled up on the cold concrete outside their cell and fell fast asleep.

"I think you boys better face it," Dave the Otter graciously informed them one day when he was seeing a new client through lockup. "Your day has come and gone. People outside just don't *care* about a couple of washed-up old troublemakers like yourselves. I mean, if I were you, I'd start getting used to prison cuisine, and finish writing my memoirs or something. You just don't have a whole lot of friends left on the outside, you dig?"

2

MEMORY ECLIPSE

For the first few years or so, Buster contented himself with following his ex-wife Sandy's blossoming commercial career in the slick magazines. Shortly after the Revolution (or what was popularly referred to by contemporary historians as the Recent Global Restructuring Program), Sandy had distinguished herself as one of the world's brightest up-and-coming supermodels. She wasn't as young or leggy as the majority of supermodels who had come before, but in her own way she managed to project a playful, sexy ambivalence that soon made her one of the most familiar faces in the heavily scented pages of magazines such as *Animal Cosmo, Animal Esquire,* and, of course, the annual swimsuit issue of *Animal Sports Illustrated.*

"It's Penguinific!" Sandy's dialogue bubble exclaimed as she lounged beside convenient swimming pools, or performed hulas on white beaches. "It's Penguilicious!" *"C'est très Penguifique!"* Or: "Why not come up and try a Penguin-brand cigarette sometime, baby?" In most of these ads Sandy was sufficiently undressed to remind Buster of all those aspects of her body he hadn't stopped thinking about in years.

Tuesday and Thursday afternoons, Charlie and Buster were let into the exercise yard to shoot hoops, pump iron, or walk in aimless circles on the weedy jogging track. On sunny days when the sky was so blue it reminded him of water, Buster couldn't get Sandy out of his mind, or stop wondering who was making love to her these days, and what his species might be. At times like these, the cold concrete walls leaned into Buster and made him edgy with adrenalin. He had to get out of here. He had to get back to Sandy.

"Charlie?"

"Huh?"

Like Rick, Charlie was growing gray around the temples and lanky around the joints. He had also gone deaf in his left ear, so Buster made sure to speak into his right.

"Do you ever think, you know, about busting out of here?"

Charlie worked a piece of straw from one side of his mouth to the other.

"To be honest, old friend, I don't guess I do."

They were sitting on a wooden bench in the exercise yard, watching Roy the Gorilla in the guard tower overhead. Roy was currently peering into the barrel of his rifle, trying to pry forth a chewing gum wrapper he'd dropped down it by accident.

" 'Cause this is like the funny thing, Charlie. It just suddenly came to me, like. You're a bird, Charlie. You could just fly the hell out of here, couldn't you? Just take wing and like *split*. I wouldn't hold it against you, you know. Just 'cause I can't fly doesn't mean I'd hold your freedom against you."

For the first time since Buster had known him, moistness fogged Charlie's bifocal lenses. He removed and wiped them against the sleeve of his cotton work shirt.

"I know you wouldn't hold my freedom against me, old pal. You're not that kind of bird, are you?"

As Charlie explained it to Buster that strange afternoon, flight was not a function of the wings, but an expression of the heart. For years now (as long as he and Buster had known each other, anyway) Charlie had lacked the fundamental psychodynamics that an act like flight required. Belief in oneself. Belief in one's world. Belief in the abilities of language and body to carry a bird into dimensions it doesn't know about.

"I wasn't walking to keep you company," Charlie confessed that night after lights out. "I was walking because I couldn't do any better. I guess I should've told you or something, but I don't know. It's sort of a difficult thing to admit. That you're a bird with wings, but you can't fly. Especially when flying's just about the only thing you ever knew how to do in the first place."

At that point, Charlie began to cry. Buster put one wing stiffly across Charlie's shoulder, feeling discomfited and meager. The sobs poured out of Charlie like rhetoric used to. His body shook and his shoulders heaved.

"Don't fall apart on me, Charlie, okay?"

Buster couldn't prevent himself from shedding a few wet, peremptory tears of his own. Suddenly he realized the incredible closeness of the walls encircling them. He could hear animals in neighboring cells, whimpering with pain, fear, and terrible remorse.

"I don't know what I'll do if you fall apart on me, Charlie. We'll figure something out, okay? One of these days, I promise. We'll get out of here and I'll look after you, okay?"

Within days of Charlie's confession, Buster began to wonder about the true animal order of things.

If flight was an ability of the heart, then why, Buster asked himself, couldn't anyone with enough heart in him fly? Even a penguin, say. Even a middle-aged, lonely penguin who had taken a few wrong turns in his life, and had suffered his share of hard knocks.

For the following eighteen months, Buster spent nearly every available moment in the exercise yard training his heart for lift off. He would stand staring straight up into the sky, beating his nubby wings against his sides with a steady, undeterrable persistence, forcing his mind to look far beyond the cold, dull realities of this public institution. The concrete spaces. The aluminum-tasting water fountain. The sludgy food and rusty communal showers. Buster would untether his mind until it drifted away into the rhythm of his own flapping, steadily flapping white-and-black wings. And in his heart, he would fly. He would lift himself into the blue sky and fly away from all the thick, meaningless reality he didn't want to know about anymore.

"I'm a good penguin," he whispered in ritual self-affirmation. "I'm a strong penguin. I'm a penguin who has fought for noble causes and dreamed noble dreams. I have heart enough. I have spirit enough. I have wings enough and more. I'm coming home to you, Sandy. I'm flying over these prison walls and coming home."

Buster returned to his cell after every failed launch attempt with a renewed modesty that was almost eloquent. Charlie, who had taken up oil painting, didn't even look up when Buster was let in by Roy and his jangly bundle of keys. He just continued mixing pigments and applying them to his pale canvases.

There are some things, he thought, a bird needs to work out for himself.

"That's nice, Charlie," Buster always said, gesturing vacantly at the spattered easel. Then Buster lay back on his cot and stared at the ceiling, wondering about the sky beyond, and how much longer it might take him to get there. Meanwhile, hanging from all the available wall space, Charlie's paintings depicted high aeronautic views of mountains, rivers, valleys, and oceans.

Sometimes they even displayed the lumpish Animal Planet in all its splendor, pear shaped and spinning softly in a universe bathed with light. There was something about Charlie's global visions that projected a soft, inner radiance Buster didn't want to look at. Charlie had been there, the paintings affirmed. To places Buster could only dream about.

"Thanks, Buster," Charlie said. He cocked his head and examined his latest work in progress from a slightly different perspective. "I don't mind this one too much myself."

They might not exchange another word or glance for the entire week. Every day they woke up, read newspapers, ate food out of stained plastic bowls, and went back to sleep.

Years passed.

The Animal Planet continued to spin.

Then one day in early spring, Roy the Gorilla brought them the good news. It was Roy's last official function before his impending retirement, and he was really going to miss all his good friends behind bars here at the prison. For his many years of dedicated service, Roy had received a free canteen lunch, a minimal State pension, and a Swatch. Buster and Charlie were sick and tired of being shown the Swatch, though, so Roy was happy about this new information he could share.

"Look, guys, you're getting paroled! Doesn't that news make you guys really happy or what?"

Neither Charlie nor Buster sat up from their bunks.

"Maybe we don't want to go," Charlie said.

Roy removed his hat, and from the hat a crumpled ball of paper. He opened the ball of paper and tried to shake it into some sort of official-looking shape.

"Look right here, Charlie. Just read that. *We the Government of the United States of Animals, do hereby forthwith with all our hearts, do hereby tell Buster and Charlie that they can go home."* Roy was running his finger across the lines of smudged laser printing as if he could really read them. "Come on, you guys! Cheer up, will you! It's Liberation Day and you've been forgiven for all your bad deeds! Isn't that what you've always wanted? To be free?"

When they stepped outside into the prison parking lot, they stood stiffly for a while, blinking at the bright white sun. Each of them had been issued a new suit of clothes, a gray cloth knapsack, and a cold tomato-and-cheese sandwich. And waiting for them at the curb was none other than Dave the Otter in a long luxury stretch limo with dark reflective windows.

"Come on, guys. Get in, will you? I haven't got all day."

When Buster and Charlie climbed onto the plush, air-conditioned leather upholstery, they found hot meals awaiting them on stainless-steel serving trays, chilled champagne in a bucket, and caviar spread thickly on soda crackers and toast.

"Drink up, guys," Dave the Otter said dully, pulling out of the parking lot onto a long, ugly industrial road. Wearing a natty blue chauffeur uniform, Dave obviously resented this latest downturn in his professional career. "You guys are being made an example of for the entire animal population. Which means you don't never have to go back to prison again no more."

As they were escorted through the endless suburbs and industrial parks of a major American city, Buster and Charlie saw entire city blocks filled with gray, nondescript warehouses and munitions factories. They saw shy, anxious children filing through metal detectors into weedy public school yards and cinema-plexes. They saw bankrupt shopping malls, dead housing tracts composed almost entirely of stucco, and billboards on every horizon, proclaiming that everything in the world was the BIGGEST, BEST, MOST BEAUTIFUL, and MOST PERFECT.

"Look at all the roads leading everywhere," Charlie said, gazing out at the same old world amazed. "Roads leading to other cities and countries. Roads leading to other roads."

There was traffic. And there were enormous eighteen-wheelers filled with produce and gadgets. And there was pollution. And there were homeless animals camped out in ruined buildings and parking lots. And there were tracts of identical houses and shopping centers and specialty stores classified according to race, gender, class, and species. Mousey Mansions. Dog Plaza Drive-in. Cat-o-Nine-Cocktails. And of course the ever-popular Pachyderm Putt-Putt Miniature Golf Course. In the last ten years or so, the world hadn't changed at all. But that didn't mean it would ever stop growing.

As they approached the city center, the buildings around them grew taller, but not much better looking. Pretty soon Dave the Otter was driving them down a long concrete ramp into the bowels of a gigantic, shadowy parking garage, and escorting them into a dark, graffiti-scrawled service elevator.

"Step right in, ladies and germs," Dave said. "Next stop is where the big boys live."

Dave punched the button for the 120th floor—EXPRESS.

And with a subterranean *whoosh,* the elevator began its long ascent.

"I'm afraid you're yesterday's news, Charlie." Bunny Fairchild was racing her stationary Exercycle down the middle of the wide, cleanly furnished penthouse apartment. Since the last time Buster and Charlie saw her, Bunny had developed bigger breasts, higher cheekbones, cuter nostrils, and a weirdly shiny complexion, as if someone had gone over her entire face with a belt sander. While her good legs pumped steadily at the Exercycle, she ate spoonfuls of Ben and Jerry's Cherry Garcia and chainsmoked a posh-looking brand of low-nicotine filter cigarettes. "Your day's come and gone, Charlie, and I hope that doesn't sound cruel or anything. But we were always straight with one another, Charlie. That's probably why we learned to respect each other so much."

Charlie couldn't remember if he'd been here before. The wide panoramic windows, though, seemed strangely familiar.

"You're an honest woman, Bunny." There wasn't a trace of irony in Charlie's voice, which caused Buster, vaguely discombobulated by the altitude, to look over. "You always tell people where they stand, and I think that's an admirable quality in any creature. Human or otherwise."

Bunny, however, had not brought Charlie here to discuss terms. She had brought him here to gloat.

"We don't want you back, Charlie. You had your chance and blew it. We just want you to know there're no hard feelings, at least not on *this* side of the fence, anyway. So once the ceremony's over, you guys are on your own; please don't call or write, okay? Oh, and by the way, are you sure you guys wouldn't like a beer or something? Or hey, there's always plenty of ice cream."

"You were a flash in the pan, Charlie," Bunny continued later after her shower. She was wearing a flimsy silk kimono and drying her short, dyed-blond hair with a green terry-cloth towel. "But our friend Mr. Big has what I call staying power. He came and went, Charlie, but then he came and went again. And then he came and went again, and again, and again, and again. One week the newspapers and magazines are oohing and ahhing about how wonderful and magnetic Mr. Big is. The next week they're yelling and bitching about what an egomaniacal, talentless phony he's become. This guy's already had more comebacks than Madonna, Sylvester Stallone, and Elvis put together. And I'm not just talking about the *first* Elvis, Charlie. I'm talking about *both* of them."

Charlie and Buster were sitting on the sofa, sharing a bottle of gaseous mineral water. While Bunny rattled on, they couldn't help gazing around themselves at all the framed portraits of former Worldco executives adorning the walls. According to their brooding, fabulous portraits, these men once strode the world like colossi. They had conquered nations, landed on the moon, defeated Communism, and made America more free.

"Which, of course, is exactly where I came in, Charlie." Bunny's voice was at once intrepid and soporific, so that every so often Buster and Charlie found themselves missing an entire train of thought. "Do you know that before I came along, Worldco used to waste an entire factory manufacturing *one* piece of merchandise for *one* demographic consumer group? They'd manufacture, say, rotary blenders for humans, and that was that. But now, ever since the brainstorm of good old *moi,* Worldco has adapted that same factory to produce numerous cost-and-material-related products for a variety of *different* consumer groups. Such as rotary blenders for rabbits. And rotary blenders for dogs. Rotary blenders for cats, mice, squirrels, left-handed pigs, and even diabetic-prone hamsters and minx. It's called *diversification,* Charlie. And you can't even *imagine* the sort of profit development it's creating for our good old friends at Worldco."

Charlie, however, wasn't trying to imagine how many different types of rotary blenders the Worldco Corporation was capable of distributing on the world market simultaneously. Instead, he was gazing up at the large, looming portrait of Worldco's current President, which hung on the west wall among crushed-velour draperies and fresh flowers in vases. During the past decade of hard, angry living, Stan Garfield had burned out his heart, liver, kidneys, lungs, urinary tract, the works. Now, according to this recent portrait, only his head remained, rigged up to a digital computer console on wheels. Oddly enough, Stan Garfield had never looked better. Or, for that matter, happier.

Charlie felt Buster give him another sharp nudge in the ribs. He looked up at Bunny, who was looking directly at him.

"Sorry if I'm boring you, Charlie. God forbid you might *learn* anything while you're here."

"God forbid," Charlie said softly.

Then Bunny escorted them both into the adjoining quarters to see how much was left of Mr. Big.

Mr. Big spent most of his time these days soaking in a large whirlpool, his gnarly limbs stretched out over the sides like collapsed banners, a tall glass of brandy awaiting his pleasure on a footstool near the toilet. Mr. Big's bathroom was littered with amber plastic vials, skin conditioners, and name-brand cosmetics. When Mr. Big wasn't imbibing all sorts of legally prescribed pharmaceuticals, he was ordering chocolate malteds and deep-fried peanut-butter-and-jelly sandwiches from his valet. Sitting in the steamy tub, his pupils dilated with the latest rage in barbiturates, Mr. Big wore a really expensive toupee that sat damply on his head like a sort of shy companion.

"Animals must unite!" Mr. Big proclaimed weakly the moment Charlie and Buster entered the room. He tried to sit up in the tub, flailing his limbs loosely. Then, with a short squeak of porcelain and a splash, Mr. Big collapsed back into his former torpor.

The engine of the whirlpool continued to drone underneath the floor.

The ceremony held later that afternoon was perfunctorily efficient, like just about everything Bunny Fairchild organized these days. After a cursory briefing, Charlie and Buster were led to a stage in the middle of the Functions Room, where they were situated at a long wooden dais aside Mr. Big and a generic corporate VP type.

"Charlie? Hi, I'm Jack O'Malley, Worldco's current Vice President in Charge of Marketing. We're sorry Stan couldn't be here personally, you know, but he was scheduled for one of his lube jobs and, well, things just don't always work out the way we'd like them to, do they? Before everything gets started, though, I just wanted to introduce myself, and say I was a big fan of yours way back there in the beginning. Before your career fizzled, of course."

"Nice to meet you, Jack."

Mr. Big, meanwhile, was so stoned he had to be propped against the dais and sedated with horse tranquilizers. He was wearing his customary black cape and a shiny chrome codpiece.

"I forgive you!" he blared every so often. "Be free and be happy! Mr. Big loves you all!"

"Not yet, honey," Bunny whispered, adjusting Mr. Big's cape over one shoulder. "Wait for the cameras, okay?"

At this point the large double doors were pulled open to admit a hoard of contrite newspeople, who kept obligingly within the assigned perimeters of a red velvet rope. Then, at Bunny's signal, they snapped a blizzard of carefully orchestrated photo ops, and were permitted to venture a series of brief, prescheduled questions.

"What will you do now, Charlie?"

222

"Where will you go?"

"Did you ever expect it would end like this, Charlie?"

"What did you think about while you were in prison? Did you ever feel any regrets?"

"Will you go back on the college lecture circuit?"

"Or will you just retire and rest on your laurels?"

Charlie smiled blankly at the cameras. Since Charlie's imprisonment, an entire new generation of reporters had taken over the reins from their forefathers. Yet, surprising enough, they didn't look or sound one bit different.

"We're going away," Charlie responded, refusing to elaborate any further. "Buster and I just want to say thanks for all your attention, but we'll be going away now, and we won't be coming back."

Bunny escorted Mr. Big to the front of the stage and gave him a hard pinch in the rump.

"Now, honey."

"You're forgiven!" Mr. Big brayed.

The necessary documents were signed and formally displayed to the cameras.

"Mr. Big pardons you for all your crimes! And now you can be free!"

OUT OF TOWN

Needless to say, Buster and Charlie didn't feel very free when the stretch limo deposited them later that afternoon at a downtown bus stop.

"Don't take any wooden nickels!" Dave the Otter called out

over his shoulder, and squealed off into the hot, smoggy traffic. "Boob brains!"

It was almost a half hour before the next city bus arrived, packed with animal peons armed to the gills with shivs, bagged lunches, and bad breath.

"I feel a little nauseous, Charlie," Buster said. "I can't tell if it's from that circus back there or from all this damn carbon monoxide."

"Hold on just a little longer," Charlie replied. "I'm getting us out of here, okay?"

They went directly to the Worldco Animal Transit Authority, where Charlie purchased two tickets on the next bus out of town. They had just enough money left over from their prison grant to buy a six-pack of cold beer.

"It's all pretty horrible, isn't it, Charlie? What a bunch of awful people run the world these days. And look what they've done to the planet, Charlie. Look what they've done to themselves. I finally understand, Charlie, I really do. I understand why you can't fly anymore. How could you ever believe in anything ever again? I know I couldn't, Charlie. I couldn't believe in anything."

Buster slept on the slow bus ride through miles of honking traffic, over swaybacked bridges, and across potholed interstates. When he awoke it was nearly morning, and Charlie was sitting up finishing a warm can of Schlitz.

"Don't go back to sleep," Charlie told him. "We're almost there."

They disembarked into a cold pale morning filled with faintly glistening stars. Out here, the country was only half ravaged by technology. One large, furrowed valley had been thoroughly exhausted by strip-mining equipment. An old chemical refinery had recently been shut down by the EPA. What little true landscape that remained contained only the wilted promise of a few green trees and a dead, grayish river.

However, there was one grassy mountain that technology hadn't gotten to yet. It was high and it was steep. Charlie began climbing it right away.

"Sometimes anger's enough," he said, plodding steadily up the mossy path, kicking soda cans and candy wrappers out of his way like St. Patrick clearing Ireland of serpents. "Because you know what's worse, don't you? Boredom, Buster. Sheer unadulterated mindless soulless rush-hour-traffic-type *boredom,* for chrissakes. When a body's bored, Buster, the blood stops circulating or something. You don't breathe right, or oxygenate properly. So being righteously *pissed off* every so often may not always be good for your state of mind, but sometimes it at least wakes you up. It makes you *do* something besides sit around feeling *sorry* for yourself all day."

Charlie was already out of breath, but Buster, well conditioned by his years of prison calisthenics, had no trouble keeping up.

"Perspective is something of a lie," Charlie said later when they'd reached the summit. They were sitting in the shade of a large brown rock, looking at the wide landscape below. "From this height, things look almost continuous, don't they, Buster? They don't look like someone's just finished murdering the soil with petro-chemicals, or chasing all the animal residents into polluted cities and lousy jobs. You can't even see most of the strip-mining scars from up here, can you, Buster? That's what perspective means, I often think. Getting so far away from things you can't see them clearly anymore."

Buster, however, was not entirely convinced.

"Maybe it just means you're looking at something bigger than the damage, Charlie. Maybe, when you get up high like this, you're looking at the whole planet, and how incredible it is, and how vast and amazing it'll always be. Isn't that what you always used to say, Charlie? That whole beautiful blue-and-green planet we belong to. That we'll always be part of it, and that it'll always be part of us, too."

When Charlie didn't respond, Buster thought he was digesting what Buster had said. After another moment, though, Buster realized he'd been speaking directly into Charlie's bad ear.

Then, quite abruptly, Charlie stood and dusted himself off.

"You know what the biggest lie of all time is, Buster? That we live our lives alone. That's what the corporate world *wants* us to think, because they want to figure human nature in terms of the good old *competitive* economy. Human beings who are always alone will try to rip each other off, and never organize, and never care about anything but how much money they make, or how much they own. But when you come right down to it, Buster, I've spent so much time with you, I don't see how we can ever be apart. Because I'll always find myself talking to you, pal, even when you're not around. And I'll always hear your voice talking back to me."

Then, without once looking back, Charlie started jogging down the hill. Perhaps he didn't want Buster to see the tears in his eyes. Or perhaps he didn't want to spoil his intense concentration.

Buster, meanwhile, felt a little rush of adrenaline.

"You can do it, Charlie," he whispered out loud, even before he knew what was happening. "I know it, Charlie. You can really *do* it."

Charlie had begun trotting awkwardly on his black, spindly legs, shaking his weak wings open, stumbling on stones and dead roots and things. He looked about as graceful as a cardboard box being dragged over the ground by a rope.

226

"You can do it, Charlie," Buster said out loud. He was getting to his feet. He was feeling the cool breeze on his face.

"What's that?" Charlie called out over his shoulder. "I can't hear you, Buster!"

Charlie was starting to work his prison-stiffened wings up and down, up and down. They seemed asynchronous, as if each was responding to a different, unrelated hemisphere of Charlie's brain. He was slipping and sliding down the flinty hillside. He didn't even seem to be picking up any speed.

"I realized something, Charlie, back when *I* was trying it, you know?" Buster was shouting into the wind. "Sometimes it's not the heart that tells the mind what it *can* do! Sometimes it's the body that tells the heart what it *must!*"

Charlie's wings were completely unfurled to reveal gray, patchy bits of frazzled feathers.

"What's that, Buster? I can't hear you, pal! I'm trying to fly!"

And at that precise moment, Buster saw Charlie for who he really was, and for who he would always be. A foolish, partially deaf, prematurely aged creature who refused to be realistic about the world. Who was running down a green knobby hill flapping his foolish, baggy wings at the wind—imagining he could fly when he could hardly even run properly anymore.

And at the moment Buster knew it was impossible, he also knew how very possible it was.

Charlie's entire body gave a little lift, as if it were being tugged upward by an invisible string.

Then he came down again and his legs buckled, spraying rocks in every direction, his tail feathers skidding him upright long enough to keep him running some more.

He was flapping harder. He was gathering momentum. And then again he was lifting off the ground, lifting off the hard descent of the hill. He was wobbling higher, gradually higher, over the trees, flying, flying, he was flying, he was flying.

"Keep going, Charlie!" Buster screamed. He was jumping up and down on the green hill. He knew anyone could do anything they ever wanted to because he had lived to see the impossible happen.

A bird flying with its own two wings! Who ever would have believed it?

"I can't hear you, Buster! I'm flying! I'm afraid to come down!"

"Don't come down, Charlie! Keep going! Keep flying! I can take care of myself!"

"What's that, Buster? I have to keep flying! I can't come down!"

Charlie was beginning to diminish into the horizon, the bright white sunlight swallowing him into a sort of ethereal foam. "Take care of yourself, Buster! Don't let the bastards get you down!"

Charlie's words were swallowed by the wide sky. And so was Charlie's black, wavering body. So small. So amazing. So high.

"I'm coming with you, Charlie!" Buster couldn't restrain himself another moment. He was flapping his nubby wings against his sides, running down the flinty hill as fast as he could. And then, before he knew it, he could feel it too. He was lifting off. He was flying—

—and then fell tumbling down the flinty hill, head over heels, crashing to a stop on a smooth, grassy ledge.

The blue sky was empty except for a few clouds. Buster wasn't certain, but he thought he could hear Charlie's voice one last time.

"I'm really *flying,* man! I really am!"

At which point Charlie's voice disappeared forever from Buster's life.

Within the next forty-five minutes or so, Buster was out on the highway, hitching a ride south.

"Don't get too many penguins in these parts." The man driving the truck was none other than Zack Marmaduke, the surly, alcoholic sailor who had given Buster and Charlie so much grief during their brief tenure as Merchant Marines. "Hey, don't I know you from somewhere, guy?"

It turned out that in the last dozen years or so, Zack had seen his share of hard luck, and was now trying to put as much of it behind him as possible.

"I know I was something of an asshole," Zack confessed over coffee at a roadside diner. "I was just so pissed off at everything, you know? I felt so stupid, and I was always broke, and of course I was boozing *constantly* back then, so things didn't get any better. I did a lot of things in those days I'm ashamed of. I'm sorry if I ever caused you and your friends any trouble."

For a while Zack had been a human supremacist. For a while after that he went to prison for beating his wife. He had worked as a barker for a topless night club, peddled cocaine to Hollywood executives, and smuggled guns to CIA-sponsored terrorists in Central America. As Zack unreeled his list of bad credits, Buster felt a little awed by him. He was amazed at how much self-degradation one puny animal life could admit to and yet still prevail.

"So then I'd get so angry, you know, and I'd drink some more, and I'd get angrier, and suddenly it was all *her* fault, you know, everything about my life, everything I had ever done wrong. It was *her* fault and I wanted to kill her, you know? And I'd knock her around, and I'd hit her, and I knew it was wrong but that just made me madder. So I hit her again. And again. I used to hate her so much, man. I used to get so angry at the sort of person she'd let me become."

They ordered more coffee, and Buster tried to ignore a tabloid on the newsrack beside the counter. He thought he recognized a picture of Sandy on the cover. But this was neither the time nor the place to talk about *her*.

"From that day forward, all I wanted to do was die. And when you get down to it, pal, dying just isn't a very acceptable choice now, is it? So then I wanted to believe in God, because maybe He could make my life bearable, and show me a way out of this horrible creature I'd become. I wanted to apologize to somebody, you know? Somebody in *authority*. Somebody who could relieve me of the awful responsibility I felt for being myself. So I went to prison services, and I watched the PTL Club on TV, and I read the Bible, and you know what I found in all those places, man? I just found, I don't know, all this *anger*. Butcher the heathens, they kept saying. Destroy the evil. Put the criminals behind bars. Hate the blacks. Hate the poor. Hate the Jews. Hate *some*one, *any*one but *yourself,* man. And let me tell you, I was tempted. I'd been down that road before. I don't know, man, maybe it was me. Maybe I'm just an angry guy or something, and they had something important to tell me, but I wouldn't listen. Anyway, I gave up on God, and with a lot more time under my belt, I gave up on hate, too. I quit drinking, got a job, and now I just get by one day at a time, as they say. . . . Oh, well, what the hell time is it, anyway? Midnight? Jesus. I got to get this rig into Dallas by tomorrow, man. Maybe we should get going, you think?"

As if Buster didn't feel awkward enough letting Zack pay the tab, he also had to bum another two bits for the tabloid.

"I owe you," Buster said, folding the paper under his wing.

"Oh forget it," Zack said. "Anyway, considering how things work out in this crazy world, maybe I actually owe *you* one. You think that's possible, huh?"

That night they drove nearly six hundred miles without stopping, listening to country music and watching the dark, moonlit agricultural fields swoop by on either side. According to the *National Enquirer,* Sandy the Penguin had pulled a Marlene Dietrich and refused to grow old in front of cameras. Despite a record-breaking contract offer from the Sears Mature Woman line of cosmetics, Sandy had converted all her savings into blue diamonds and disappeared into the frozen Antarctic without leaving so much as a forwarding address. She still had family out there, she frequently explained in public interviews. And some things, she explained just as often, are more important than money.

In the morning Zack pulled into a roadside truckstop, where enormous eighteen-wheelers sat slumbering in the thin dawn like gentle pachyderms. Only a few miles from the Gulf, Zack had decided to sleep through the rush-hour traffic and get a fresh start after breakfast. While Zack snored away in a bed cabin behind the seats, Buster quietly rolled up his spare clothes in the tabloid newspaper and climbed down from the truck.

Out here the sun was gigantic and white, and in the silver streak of sky between sun and mountains, Buster thought he saw a black bird flying west, into the morning. Not performing cartwheels or anything fancy, just flying intrepidly onward, to places where day led into night, and night led into day again.

"There should be a sign, Charlie," Buster said, as he walked down the long whizzing highway to the sea. "And that sign should be posted on the edge of our planet, so it's the first thing anybody sees when they get here. And that sign should say this:"

WELCOME TO ANIMAL PLANET,
WHATEVER TYPE OF ANIMAL YOU ARE.
PLEASE TRY TO GET ALONG WITH EVERYBODY WHILE YOU'RE HERE.
IT'S THE ONLY PLANET WE'VE GOT.

Then, swinging his bundle over one shoulder, Buster carried on down the highway, ignoring the honks and jeers of passing motorists and wondering how long the clean blue sky would last.

He could already smell the ocean from here.

And he could hardly wait.

231